A NECKTIE FOR GIFFORD

The bounty hunter known as 'Montero' learns that his brother is to be hanged for murder in the New Mexico town of Alamagordo. A single clue left by the dead man — the two letters 'MA' — ensures that a guilty verdict is inevitable. The two brothers had parted some years before under hostile circumstances, but Montero is convinced that Mace Gifford would never shoot a man in the back. He plans an ingenious escape, but saving his brother's neck is only the beginning — he has to find the real killer . . .

Books by Ethan Flagg
in the Linford Western Library:

TWO FOR TEXAS
DIVIDED LOYALTIES
DYNAMITE DAZE
APACHE RIFLES
DUEL AT DEL NORTE
OUTLAW QUEEN
WHEN LIGHTNING STRIKES
PRAISE BE TO SILVER

ETHAN FLAGG

A NECKTIE FOR GIFFORD

Complete and Unabridged

LINFORD
Leicester

First published in Great Britain in 2012 by
Robert Hale Limited
London

First Linford Edition
published 2014
by arrangement with
Robert Hale Limited
London

A catalogue record for this book is available from the British Library.

ISBN 978–1–4448–1994–6

Published by
F. A. Thorpe (Publishing)
Anstey, Leicestershire

Set by Words & Graphics Ltd.
Anstey, Leicestershire
Printed and bound in Great Britain by
T. J. International Ltd., Padstow, Cornwall

This book is printed on acid-free paper

1

Ticking Clock

Sprawled on his bunk, the prisoner gave the appearance of a desolate figure. The smell of his own excrement wafted from the overflowing bucket in the corner of the cell. By now he had got used to the vile odour. What did it matter anyway. He was due to be hanged in the morning.

He raised his head and peered up at the sun's shadow beaming in through the barred window. Slow yet inevitable, it moved across the stained adobe wall, a ticking clock eating away at his last hours of life on this earth. Other prisoners had scrawled their own time of incarceration, each mark signifying another day passed before the final call to pay their dues.

One erudite pensmith had scratched

a brief ode that struck a grim chord with the prisoner. It made his skin crawl with trepidation.

The final walk, the swaying noose
The Reaper's finger beckons.
No time to think, no time for tears.
A life snuffed out in seconds!

Unless a miracle occurred, that would be his fate. At the age of twenty-three years, a life barely started. To end up swinging at the end of a rope for a crime he hadn't committed. It all seemed so unfair.

The young man's eye was drawn to a scuttering across the far wall. A lizard paused for an instant to survey the grubby room's incumbent. Its tail flicked disdainfully as if to imply that it was now his turn to assume a superior status.

'Hope you appreciate how lucky you are, fella,' grunted the prisoner.

There was no doubt that Mace Gifford had slipped down the pecking order of life. The creature cockily sauntered towards the freedom of the open window.

But nothing in life, or death, is ever that simple.

Suddenly, fate took a grim hand in the bizarre proceedings. A hawk plunged down out of the blue and scooped up the tasty treat, which disappeared down its gullet. Law of the jungle.

The incident did nothing to raise the prisoner's mood. He could see no way of defeating the avaricious appetite of the Grim Reaper. Just like the shadow on the wall. The sands of time were relentlessly dribbling away.

Rheumy eyes gazed blankly at the wall of his cell.

Some time later his morbid reflections were interrupted by a steady tapping outside in the prison yard.

Standing on the bunk he peered out of the window, only to woefully observe the means of his departure from this mortal coil. The grim structure stood at the far side of the prison yard.

Two carpenters worked on the sturdy gallows which dominated the enclosed yard. Only the tops of adjacent buildings could be seen poking above the high adobe walls. The territorial governor of New Mexico had only recently passed an ordinance that future hangings were to be conducted in private.

The primitive ways of the frontier were slowly being tamed as the whole country moved towards a new era of civilization. Respect and consideration for the individual were the new by-words. And the governor wanted his patch to become worthy of statehood.

One step towards earning that prestigious distinction would be to do away with the more brutal aspects of legal executions. Public hangings had become popular spectacles more akin to wild saloon shindigs than the sombre occasions they were meant to be.

In consequence, the official hangman now had to be present to oversee the proceedings and accord the condemned felon a dignified and swift departure.

One of the men repairing the gallows noticed the pale face peering out of the cell window. He nudged his partner, then shouted across to the watching prisoner.

'Gotta make sure that neck of your'n gets snapped off clean as a whistle,' he jeered. A broad grin spread across the workman's leering visage. 'We can't have the state hangman reportin' us for shoddy work, now can we?'

His buddy nodded in agreement. Then, evincing a slow and deliberate relish, he hauled back the lever to allow the trap to swing down. A hollow thud, ominous and terminal echoed across the yard.

'Yep, Charlie,' he averred in mock seriousness. 'Seems to be workin' just fine now.'

Charlie Boggs added an extra squirt of grease to the hinges as the two men gathered up their tools.

'Pity they now have to conduct these

hoohahs in private,' Biff Ryker commented, shaking his head. 'Takes all the fun out of it. Now we won't be able to see the results of our good work.'

'At least they're gonna display the bastard's corpse outside the council offices afterwards for everybody to see,' commented Charlie Boggs. A mirthless snigger followed the cutting remark. 'Then we'll be able to give it a good kickin'.'

'And I heard there's gonna be free drinks at the Golden Nugget as well,' said Ryker, slinging the tool bag nonchalantly over his left shoulder with a laugh.

'See yuh at the party then, Gifford.'

'Guess we'll enjoy it more'n you,' came the parting witticism from Boggs as the two men left the yard.

Taunting bites of laughter bounced off the wall of the dirty cell as the prisoner slumped back down on to his bunk.

How had it come to this? To be accused of a crime of which he was totally innocent, and now waiting to be hanged for it.

The sun's shadow still crept steadily across the walls, bringing Mace Gifford closer to his own necktie party as he mused on the events that had brought him to this sorry plight.

* * *

It had all started a month previously, following Gifford's release from the territory's principal jail-house in Santa Fe. He had served his two years for robbing a stagecoach on the Cimarron cut-off. Drifting south he had arrived in Alamagordo with barely enough dough to buy a meal, let alone afford a bed in the cheapest flophouse.

His pockets were empty apart from a lonely silver dollar. It was the last of five given to every convict by the prison governor upon their release. The other four had been spent on the purchase of a second-hand Navy Colt pistol and ammunition. He had survived by helping out on ranches for bed and board.

Tying up his jaded mount outside the Golden Nugget saloon, he extricated the dollar piece and peered down at it.

What should he spend it on? A hearty meal sounded good as his empty stomach rumbled. Then the ribald laughter and tinkle of lively music coming from the nearby saloon drew his attention. Or maybe a last chance to raise some serious dough on the roulette wheel?

He tossed the coin, watching it spin like a twinkling star against the twilight backdrop of early evening.

'Heads for the bright lights,' he mumbled aloud.

He caught the falling coin and surveyed the depiction. Heads it was. Shoulders lifted in a weary shrug, he made to step up on to the boardwalk.

* * *

'Got a visitor for you.'

The gruff announcement jerked the

prisoner out of his morbid ruminations. So intent had he been on nursing the waves of self pity that the opening of the door giving access to the cellblock had gone unnoticed.

He looked up.

Standing outside the barred door was a young girl of no more than eighteen years. She was holding a tray. A thin wispy creature, she possessed that aura of innocence and vulnerability that excited some men. As a result she had been snapped up by May Belle Sumner, the gregarious madam who ran the Red Garter cathouse.

Ellie Spavin had soon become a favourite.

She was the only person in town who felt any sympathy for the condemned man. That was because he had stood up for her when two drunken roughnecks had tried to have their way with her down a back alley behind the bordello.

The incident happened just before he had entered the Golden Nugget saloon following his arrival in Alamagordo.

Ellie was a new employee and rather green as to the goings-on that such an establishment pursued. The money was very good but having to satisfy the rampant needs of drunken cowpokes was degrading and obnoxious to the young girl. She had therefore determined to seek employment elsewhere.

This was to be her last night at the Red Garter.

May Belle ran a strict but well-ordered bagnio. She always insisted that money up front was a priority before clients could participate in the variety of licentious activities on offer. The well-upholstered madam was sorry to be losing Ellie. The kid was a good money-spinner.

Two jaspers had just been thrown out after trying to force their way inside under the pretext of settling up on payday. The heavyweight bouncer wasted no time in ejecting them.

Ellie had come outside later that evening for a breath of air between clients.

The two disgruntled men had spotted her and figured on enjoying a freebie. Their bumbling advances having been repelled, a far more brutal assault on the young woman had then taken place.

Screams of pain had drawn Mace down the narrow cut where he had discovered the sordid affair.

'Let her alone!' he hissed.

The odious duo paused in their assault. Baleful scowls were aimed at the unwelcome intruder.

'Wait your turn, mister.' slurred one of the attackers. 'You can have her when we're finished and not afore.'

Mace didn't bother with a reply.

A swift clout round the ear from his revolver had dispatched the gurgling speaker. The other had immediately pulled a knife. The bushwhacker released the girl and lunged at his assailant. But drink had slowed his reactions and he overbalanced, tumbling on to his back.

Mace took full advantage of the situation. As he drove his boot into the guy's flailing arm the knife flew off into the dark. A couple of savage punches to the jaw effectively terminated any further retaliation.

'You OK, miss?' he enquired of the shocked girl. A brief nod followed as the girl covered her exposed body with the remnants of a torn dress.

Mace grabbed the stunned thug by his shirt and dragged him upright. He drew back a bunched fist, ready to continue the punishment should the critter show any signs of resistance.

He need not have worried. Biff Ryker had had enough.

'Now get this piece of dung outa here fast afore I lose my temper,' Mace rapped, jabbing a thumb towards the recumbent Charlie Boggs. 'And if'n I come across you yeller bellies again' — he poked a meaningful finger into the chest of the bleary-eyed Ryker — 'then you best watch out.'

Ryker quickly hauled his buddy up and stumbled away.

Mace escorted the shaken girl back into the relative safety of the bordello before returning to the main street. He checked to make certain that the two bushwhackers were not around.

In his pocket that silver dollar was still itching to be put to good use. The Golden Nugget's enticing promise was drawing him like a moth to a flame.

2

Framed

Mace pushed open the batwings and entered the fetid den of iniquity. He paused just inside the door to survey the room.

The place was full to bursting. But nobody gave the trail-worn drifter a second glance. Too intent was everybody on pursuing their own pleasures. Men sat round green baize tables playing card games, mainly poker. At the far end was the game that Gifford sought — the roulette table.

He weaved a path through the swaying crowd and changed his dollar for small-denomination wooden playing chips. The cashier gave the unkempt player a look of scornful disdain. But the mocking regard bounced off the newcomer. All that interested him was joining the other gamblers.

For a half-hour he played the wheel. Lady Luck seemed to be smiling down on him. The small heap of chips grew steadily. When the ex-con eventually called it a day he had amassed almost $300.

The cashier was now all unctuous flattery as the jaunty gambler carelessly tossed him a ten-dollar bill from his winnings.

He celebrated his new-found wealth with a few drinks at the bar. When he stumbled over to the door with the intention of booking a room at the swankiest hotel in town a silky voice penetrated the drink-sozzled mush of his brain.

'Fancy a few hands of poker, mister?'

Mace lurched to a halt. He clutched at the batwings to steady himself.

Poker? Though Mace was not usually a gambling man his brother Clem Gifford had taught him the rudiments of the game before the two went their separate ways. Maybe a couple of hands would round off the night with a flourish. After all, wasn't Lady Luck watching over him tonight?

He cast a glassy eye towards the speaker. An oily smile was pasted on to the skeletal features of a nattily dressed card-wielder. A beaverskin derby was perched on his bullet head at a rakish angle.

'Sure,' Mace drawled. 'Why not?'

The man rose from his seat and ushered his new victim to a chair.

And so the game proceeded. As time passed luck certainly appeared to be continuing to favour the greenhorn gambler. His stack of chips mounted, much to the consternation of Luke Torrance. Beads of sweat broke out over the gambler's forehead. This was not how it was meant to be. His waxed moustache twitched with barely suppressed anger.

But Honest Luke, as he liked to be known, was not beaten yet. A devious glint sparked in his narrowed gaze. All too soon the tables had been turned.

Mace's stack of chips began to disappear.

When the gambler leaned over to rake in yet another winning pot Mace tottered to his feet. He kicked back his chair and grabbed for the old Navy stuck in his belt.

'You cheatin' tinhorn!' he yelled. 'I saw you deal that last card from the bottom of the deck. There's only one way of handling skunks like you.' The hammer of the revolver snapped back. The gun pointed as the other players dived for cover before the lead started to fly.

But the Golden Nugget was prepared for such outbursts.

Two vigilant minders suddenly appeared through the dense fug of yellow smoke. One slung an arm around Mace's neck, dragging him back, while the other wrestled the gun from his hand. During the mêlée the pistol exploded. But the bullet dug harmlessly into the wall.

The two saloon toughs hustled Mace outside into the back alley where a couple of well-placed thwacks from a billycock laid him out cold.

The next thing he remembered was waking up in a small room ensconced in a feather bed. Where was he? And how had he got here?

The mystery was further compounded when a girl entered the room carrying a mug of coffee. It was the very girl whom he had rescued earlier that evening. She quickly took in his bewildered expression.

'Glad you've finally come round,' she murmured, dabbing his face with a damp cloth. The injured man winced. His head felt like it had been kicked by a loco mule. 'Drink this.' She handed him the steaming mug. 'It'll make you feel better.'

He didn't get a chance to sample the drink. A vigorous rapping on the door was followed by a stentorian demand for it to be opened.

'This is the marshal,' hollered an irate voice. 'You have a jasper in there who's wanted for murder. Best open this door now afore I bust it down.'

Both occupants stared at one another. They were stunned into immobility. The baffled expression on Mace Gifford's face indicated that he was just as bewildered by this grim turn of events as was the girl.

Without any further explanation he was hustled away by the town marshal and his deputy.

Slung into the hoosegow, Mace found himself accused of shooting the gambler with whom he had so recently had an altercation.

His trial took place a week later, where it emerged that Honest Luke Torrance had tried to identify his assailant by writing the name in the dust at the rear of the saloon. But all he had managed were the two letters **MA** before he succumbed to the two bullet wounds in his back.

MACE had obviously been the intended name, since he had earlier threatened to get even with the gambler. It was an open and shut case.

The jury were out less than an hour, after which a unanimous guilty verdict was brought. No amount of pleading innocence by the defendant had swayed the twelve good men and true.

After all, who else could have shot the guy? Numerous witnesses came forward to testify that Honest Luke was regarded as a fair dealer who gave everyone an even break. And the accused was the only person in town having those two damning letters at the start of his name.

* * *

Once again Mace heard the irate tones of the short-fused marshal. This time the prisoner was seated on a hard cot in the smelly cellblock.

'Don't just stand there, girl,' snorted the impatient lawdog. 'Push that tray through the hatch.' Then to the prisoner he snapped. 'And don't think there's a hidden weapon under that cloth. I've searched it. And sampled the grub at the same time.' Milton Brewer smacked his lips in appreciation. 'Much too good for the likes of you.'

'Ain't yer gonna allow us a moment of privacy, Marshal?' pleaded Mace, taking hold of the tray. 'You know that Ellie ain't trying to smuggle a gun in here. So there's no chance of a last-minute escape bein' hatched, is there?'

Milt Brewer huffed some, then reluctantly acquiesced.

'You got five minutes. No more,' he said. 'And I'm leaving the cellblock door open. Just in case.' Then he departed, leaving the couple alone.

They held hands through the bars. Their relationship could not be classed as a love affair. What was the point? Mace would be just a memory in a couple of days. And Ellie was a comely young girl with her whole life ahead of her.

Yet still they both clung to the notion that it was all a dream. Mace was innocent. A last-minute reprieve would arrive and he would be released.

But deep down they knew it was a pipe dream, an illusion. The die was cast. Justice, however misguided, would be carried through.

There was little that could be said. Mace played with his meal listlessly while Ellie looked on. Understandably he had no appetite. Trembling smiles passed between them. Fingers gingerly touched. This was the only real contact they had been afforded, or ever would manage.

Ellie had offered her services to this knight in a shabby leather vest following the rescue. But Mace had declined, not wishing to take advantage of a vulnerable lady in such fraught circumstances.

'You'll not forget me, will yuh, Ellie?' The faltering words from the distraught prisoner emerged as little more than a hoarse croak.

'Of course I won't. How could you think such a thing.' Tears trickled down the girl's smooth cheeks.

More sorrowful platitudes were passed

back and forth. Mace knew that at least there was one person in Alamagordo who cared about his passing, who would remember him with affection, at least for a short period. It was a comfort, something to cling on to during the final hours.

All too soon the brief interlude came to an end. Marshal Brewer hawked a lump of phlegm into the spittoon. The unwelcome presence of the lawman announced that the visit was over.

3

El Camaleon

Round about the same time that Mace Gifford arrived in Alamagordo, a bounty hunter going by the handle of Montero was heading south-east across the arid wasteland of the Cornudas Plateau. He had been dogging the trail of the killer known as El Camaleon for the last month. Each time the hunter figured to have caught up with the infamous Mexican outlaw the slippery varmint had somehow eluded him.

Maybe this time he would have more luck.

A loose-lipped bartender in the town of Mesquite had told him that the outlaw had left the previous day, heading south-east. Having an intimate knowledge of the terrain, Montero knew that the killer would have to stop over at the Cabrio trading post to replenish his supplies.

If the bounty hunter were to miss him again, the wily varmint would be able to slip back over the border into Mexico. And Montero would lose a hefty reward.

Montero was a determined man-hunter, one of a unique breed, who operated on both sides of the law. Although despising these relentless trackers, the authorities depended on them to bring in those felons who were causing most trouble. Skunks like El Camaleon, who was wanted for the cold-blooded slaying of at least ten people across the territory.

The varmint was a master of disguise, hence his nickname. A strutting banker one day, a persuasive snake-oil drummer another. That was why he had escaped the grasping hands of the law for so long.

Montero was not prepared to let that situation continue unchallenged.

On this occasion, luck was with him.

A watery moon pushed out just enough pale light for the hunter to maintain a steady trot through the clutching stands of catclaw and sagebrush.

As dawn broke across the scalloped outlines of the Organ Mountains, he crested a low ridge. The eastern sky was shot through with a myriad of colours as the new day struggled to assert itself. As each minute passed nature's paintbrush captured a dynamic tableau.

But the dust-caked trail rider paid it no heed. He drew his jaded mount to a halt and rubbed the grittiness from his eyes. Down below at a crossroads stood the well-known trading post. Cabrio was instantly recognizable from the flock of goats grubbing about in the rubbish near by. That was how the place had acquired its name.

It was run by a shifty character called Eli Penrose who was suspected of selling hard liquor to the Apache tribes in the vicinity. El Camaleon would be at home in such an establishment.

Montero's lean features broke into a

gratified smile when he saw the lone horse tied up outside. He would recognize that mottled grey anywhere. Now that he was sure that his quarry was inside, the pursuer could relax, at least for the moment while he figured out his next move.

He hooked out a sack of Bull Durham, rolled a stogie and lit up. The thin tube helped concentrate his thoughts, a vital stimulant when he was planning how best to deal with a cunning brigand of the Chameleon's notoriety.

The hunter's brow furrowed.

The Mexican would be no easy target. He pulled out the Wanted dodger from his saddle pack and peered down at the well-thumbed picture. A stubbled face stared back. Hard, close-set eyes beneath beetling brows gave the killer a reptilian cast, cold-blooded and merciless, like an angry sidewinder.

But Montero had the element of surprise on his side. The wanted felon would figure that, being so close to the border, he was home and dry. His guard would be down. The two gunslingers had never met. That was a distinct advantage for Montero.

The bounty hunter nodded. A thin smile of satisfaction creased his craggy visage. He had the edge. And the critter was worth a cool three grand.

Dead or Alive!

Where a hard-boiled skunk like this greaser was concerned, the hunter harboured few doubts that it would be the former. Men like the Chameleon did not surrender without a fight. One or other of them would die in the process. And Montero had no intention of its being him.

He nudged the paint mare down the slope. When still some distance from the trading post he dismounted. Leaving the horse behind a clump of ocotillo, he made his way round in a wide arc so as to approach the log building from the rear.

The barn, which also served as a blacksmith's shop was, he was thankful to see, empty. A loud snoring from above brought a loose smile to the hunter's face. The smith was clearly sleeping off the effects of a hard drinking session. Montero held little hope that his quarry would be similarly inebriated.

In ten minutes he was in position outside the back door.

Tentatively he raised the latch and it swung open silently. The hunter gave a sigh of relief, then stepped back outside.

A series of hoots akin to those of a desert owl drifted on the early-morning thermals. Within seconds the paint hove into view. Galloping at full pelt, it charged into the fenced corral, scattering the goats in all directions. Their panic-stricken bleating added to the general cacophony.

It provided the perfect distraction to enable Montero to catch the wanted outlaw on the hop.

Soundlessly, Montero cat-footed through the back room and into the main body of the trading post. To his left was a counter that acted as saloon bar and display fixture. All manner of goods were stacked on shelves behind. Tables and chairs were ranged on the other side.

There were only two occupants, both on their feet and moving towards the front window to discover the source of the rumpus. Penrose opened the door and stepped outside.

The other man, sporting a large sombrero that effectively concealed his face, was more wary. He always viewed with suspicion any unusual occurrence. Gun in hand, he hesitated before moving forward.

'Just stay right where you are, Camaleon,' rasped a gritty voice to his rear. The bandit halted, his whole body tensed up. 'Now drop that hogleg and raise your hands,' came the brusque order. 'And no tricks. I wanna take you in alive.'

As expected, the Mexican made no move to comply.

'I do not think so, *hombre*,' he

chirped in that lyrical cadence that revealed neither anger nor alarm. The sly critter made to turn round, still holding the gun.

'Stay where you are!' snapped the hunter.

The outlaw obeyed.

'So what happens now?' he warbled, a mirthless grin warping his sallow features. Then he laughed. 'Why do we not have a drink and sort this out like good *amigos*, eh? Whatever the bounty on my head, I will double it. Just for you. What you say? Is it a deal?'

Again he made to turn round. But Montero knew perfectly well that the devious skunk was playing for time, waiting his opportunity to gain the upper hand.

'No deal, scumbag,' rasped the hunter. 'I'm taking you in. Either sitting in the saddle or lying across it. Your choice. Now drop that gun or I'll make the decision for you.'

'It is a great pity that you should think this way, *señor*,' drawled the

Mexican, choosing to ignore the order. 'You and I could become partners — '

'Not a chance,' snapped the hunter.

The killer's bullet head shook in mock regret. 'Oh well, a man can but try. Now, at least tell me who has tracked me down?'

'They call me Montero,' the hunter replied impatiently. He jabbed the pistol at the Mexcican owlhoot's broad back. 'Now quit stalling, buster. My trigger finger's getting a mite itchy.'

'Ah! *Sí, sí*. The great Montero. Your reputation is well known in these parts.' The fugitive was truly impressed. 'And they say you always get your man. I am indeed honoured to have such a *hombre célebre* come after me.'

An ominous silence followed this declaration.

Then, barely above a whisper, the infamous bandit hissed, 'But today, it is I who will be riding away.'

Without any warning his left arm swept back, sending a stack of tinned peaches at the hovering bounty hunter.

At the same time he flung his burly frame to one side, scrambling behind an upturned table. Orange tongues of flame spat from Montero's gun.

Smoke filled the small room. But he had been suckered. And the slugs, missing their intended target, smashed a pair of holes in a keg of beer. Fountains of brown liquid spurted forth.

The outlaw was not slow in retaliating.

His own gun drove the hunter back behind a heavy oak cabinet. Numerous shots were fired, the exchange lasting no more than a few seconds. Then came a lull as the combatants quickly reloaded.

Montero damned himself for being hoodwinked. As he gingerly peered out from behind the cabinet, an unexpected sight greeted his ogling peepers. One that he would never have expected. Eli Penrose was creeping up behind the bandit. A large frying pan clutched in both hands, was raised above his head.

To give Eli a chance, Montero called out to distract the felon. 'Might as well surrender, you ain't got a hope in Hades of leaving here alive.'

'I would not be so sure of that, *hombre*.' Two shots rang out to emphasize the bandit's determination to escape justice.

Then a heavy clang resonated through the building as ironware connected with bone. A dull thud followed as the outlaw's body tumbled to the hard-packed earthen floor. He was laid out cold.

Penrose dropped the heavy pan, staggered over to the bar and poured himself a generous measure of whiskey. He sank it in a single gulp with no visible effect. Another quickly followed before he was able to speak.

'Never thought I'd ever get the drop on El Camaleon like that,' he muttered. He dragged in a deep lungful of air.

Montero was certain that the sly proprietor had not intervened on his behalf out of pure magnanimity.

He was right.

'I'd say that savin' your hide is worth a half-share of the bounty on this critter's head, don't yuh think?' The leering toad pushed the bottle across the bar. 'Let's drink on it, fella. Cos if I hadn't butted in when I did, you would have ended up chewing lead. I've seen this varmint in action. And believe me, he ain't no pushover.'

Montero believed him.

'I'll see that you get what's coming,' he assured Penrose, clinking glasses. 'Soon as I deliver him to the law in Las Cruces.'

The bounty hunter was certainly beholden to the crafty trader, but not to the tune of half his reward.

'You from around these parts?' asked Penrose. The hovering critter laid down a plate of hot beef chilli and a hunk of bread on the table.

'Got me a place up in the Sacramentos,' Montero replied unthinkingly. Too late he realized the indiscretion of the remark, and quickly added: 'Although I ain't hung out there for some time.'

The hasty extenuation was noted by the wily cove, who was a past master at extracting information from his dubious customers. Such apparently innocent comments always came in useful.

'Enjoy the grub,' he said brightly, and moved away as if nothing untoward had taken place.

While shovelling down the food the hunter examined the gleaming Colt pistol that he had taken from the unconscious prisoner. He had heard rumours about this gun which was said to be a new design that would change the face of gunplay. Thus far they had been issued only to lawmen. Hence the name Peacemaker.

The hunter smiled. That must be how El Camaleon had acquired his.

He hefted the gun in his hand. It felt comfortable, robust and well constructed. It was a single-shot revolver, but incorporated all-in-one shells: much better than the old cap-and-ball types he was used to. The old Navy Colt had served him faithfully, but it was no match for the Peacemaker.

Within the hour, the captive was securely tethered to his own mount with Montero leading the way back up the trail.

'You make sure to come back this way, and soon,' hollered Penrose to his disappearing back. 'Remember, I got friends in your business.'

Although he had heard the thinly veiled threat, the rider chose to ignore it. He would deal with any challenges to his continued good health as and when they occurred.

* * *

Trekking back through the pipelike formations of the towering Organ Mountains needed extra care, not only because of the jagged crags and pinnacles that attempted to spear the passing clouds.

At one crucial point the wily El Camaleon had tried to bundle the hunter off the narrow trail down a ravine. But Montero was wise to such tricks. As a punishment for the sneaky manoeuvre the outlaw spent the rest of that day trussed face down across his saddle.

At last, after they had been two days on the trail, the sleepy town of Las Cruces hove into view.

Dozing in the afternoon sun the discordant array of mud-coloured adobe buildings offered a stark contrast to the greenery. The fertile land that surrounded the town was watered by the mighty Rio Grande.

Las Cruces had grown to prominence on a crossroads. As such it had become an important trading centre. The Butterfield stage company had taken advantage of the town's position by making it their principal base of operations in the south west.

Montero would be glad to hand over the troublesome bandit to the law. Then, after collecting his payout, he intended heading for California and a well-deserved vacation. A loose smile of anticipation played across his seamed features as he nudged the paint towards the settlement.

A freight wagon passed, driven by a gnarled old teamster who gave the roped outlaw more than a passing glance. He hawked a lump of phlegm at the sneering Mexican. Only the previous month, El Camaleon had passed himself off as a wealthy Mexican trader.

Following some shady negotiations hard cash had changed hands between the participants. Then he and his gang had stolen the wagons, killing two of the drivers and retrieving the dough.

'You make sure that bastard swings good and high,' hollered the angry teamster. 'And dance on his body afterwards.'

The hunter merely nodded and continued on his way.

The county sheriff's office was halfway down the main street on the left.

Morgan Phelps was an old sparring partner. The two men had crossed swords on numerous occasions in the past. A grudging respect existed between them. Certainly not friendship, it was nonetheless a tacit understanding that they were both on the same side, even if their methods tended on occasion to clash.

The lawman was lounging in a chair outside his office. He levered himself out of the comfortable seat and stepped down to meet the dust-stained duo.

'Glad to see you managed to run this critter down,' he observed as the hunter dismounted. 'I've been after him for the last six months.'

'You ain't the only one, Morg,' replied Montero, handing the reins to the sheriff. 'Pity I beat you to it. That's a mighty handsome reward they're paying for his ugly carcass.'

Phelps gave a noncommittal grunt. That was one feature of being an authorized lawman that rankled. No matter how many felons he brought in, his share of the reward money was a pittance compared with that paid to unofficial hunters like Montero, who were able to scoop the whole caboodle.

Montero removed his wide-brimmed hat and slapped the trail dust from his garb. Then he stepped up on to the boardwalk and casually surveyed the array of Wanted dodgers pinned to the noticeboard. It was a habit. But on this occasion only something special would have persuaded him to forgo the much-anticipated trip to California.

'Anything been happening that would interest me?' he enquired.

Phelps shrugged. 'Nothing much,' the tough lawman replied, manhandling the captive into the jailhouse. 'Unless you count the hanging up at Alamagordo that's due to be carried out next week.'

The hunter was only half-listening. He had no interest in detouring to celebrate the dispatch of a felon whose capture was not of his doing. Idly he asked, 'Whose the lucky guy?'

'Some hothead called Gifford.' Phelps slammed the cellblock door shut. Then he poured two mugs of coffee and handed one to his visitor. The sheriff's face was turned away while he replaced the heavy iron pot on the stove, which meant he failed to notice the blood drain from Montero's face. The hunter's mouth had dropped open with shock.

But he quickly recovered. Shaking off the numbing effect of the blunt revelation, he forced his response to remain cool and detached.

'Would that be Mace Gifford?' he queried, forcing a blunt-edged hardness into the question.

'That's the one,' said Phelps. He lit a cigar and opened the large safe to extract the reward money. 'They say he shot and killed a gambler in the back after claiming he was cheated in a poker game.' Phelps didn't look up from his task of counting the greenbacks when he asked. 'You acquainted with this jasper?'

Montero swallowed before replying. As a result the lawman failed to observe the ashen look pasted across the hunter's taut features.

'Our trails crossed a ways back.' Montero didn't elaborate. For obvious reasons it had to remain a secret that the man due to be hanged was in fact . . . his younger brother.

The bounty hunter's real name was Clem Gifford.

4

Family Schism

With his vacation now on hold, Clem was anxious to hit the trail.

He knew that some kind of rescue attempt had to be made to prevent his brother's neck being stretched. Mace was a wild hothead for sure. Clem was not in the least surprised to learn that the kid had got himself into a fix. Nonetheless, he just couldn't bring himself to believe that his own kin was capable of gunning a man down in the back.

A half-hour later, with saddle-bags well provisioned, his horse fed and watered, the hunter left Las Cruces and headed west. That was the opposite direction he needed to take for Alamagordo. But it was vital for him to convince Phelps that the hanging was of no interest to him.

Once his brother had been freed the whole territory would be alerted. It would not help if the lawman reported that the infamous bounty hunter known as Montero had been last seen heading that way.

A plan had quickly formed inside Clem's head. The fact that an official hangman was heading towards Alamagordo from his most recent assignment in Truth or Consequences had given him an idea.

Two days' hard riding and he should be able to head the guy off at Trinity Pass in the San Andres Mountains. Then he could carry out the crucial part of his plan.

He nudged the paint to a gentle trot for two miles until Las Cruces was out of sight. Then he left the trail to head north, pushing the horse to a leg-stretching canter. He needed to be at the pass by noon of the following day if he were to have any chance of waylaying the unsuspecting executioner.

As the sturdy horse ate up the miles, Clem's thoughts drifted back to the last time he had seen his brother. The recollection drew forth a louring frown chock full of angst. It had not been a joyous occasion.

In truth, their parting had been bitter and acrimonious.

After their father had died following a cholera outbreak, young Mace Gifford had expected the farm in Missouri to be his as of right. After all, hadn't he been the one who stayed home to run the place when his elder brother had left to seek his fortune in the goldfields of South Dakota?

He'd slogged his guts out in all weathers when old Shadrack Gifford had fallen ill. Surely that counted for something?

Apparently not.

Clem had always been Pa's favourite. The younger brother ought to have known the farm would be left to him. It was traditional among the settlers that the eldest son always inherited the land.

But Mace had clung to the hope that in this case things would be different.

When those aspirations failed to materialize, Mace felt that he had been betrayed. He sank into a deep fit of depression and self-pity which quickly grew into a seething hatred for his elder kin.

There was only one way to expunge the demons that threatened to overwhelm his anguish and drive him crazy.

Revenge!

That meant getting rid of the impediment that stood in the way of his attaining his just deserts.

Clem Gifford had received word in Deadwood from the family attorney that his father had died and left the farm to him. After selling off his claim at a good profit, a letter was immediately dispatched to his brother, announcing his return.

Had the seething young hothead waited for his brother's arrival so as to discuss the matter, he would have learned that Clem had no interest in farming the land. He had struck lucky in Deadwood with a rich claim. His intention was to hand over the whole caboodle, lock, stock and barrel, for Mace to run as he saw fit.

But the younger Gifford was eaten up with vengeful thoughts. His whole being festered with a vindictive need for retaliation. A plan was hatched to get rid of Clem. But he had to make it look like an accident.

On the day of Clem's intended arrival back at the farm the simmering avenger had his scheme ready for execution. An anticipatory musing brought a grim smile to the kid's grimacing features.

He had positioned himself in the barn but towards the rear. The door was open, giving a wide view of any approaching rider. Around noon the sound of galloping hoofs assailed his ears. His whole body tensed. This was it. The moment either to go out and greet his estranged kin, or stay put and carry out his terminal scheme of retribution.

He remained hidden. Clem had to be eradicated.

The elder Gifford drew his mount to a halt and dismounted.

A large baying wolfhound bounded from the open barn door. It came to a shuddering halt before the new arrival. The snarling anger fizzled out as the dog eyed the newcomer. Its nose sniffed the air, the bared teeth were covered. The old dog's head leaned to one side, a canine look of puzzlement etched across the grizzled features.

Then its tail began to wag vigorously. Even after all this time, the hound recognized its old master's personal smell.

'Glad there's somebody here to welcome me home,' Clem said, ruffling the dog's ragged grey coat. 'You seen anything of that wayward brother of mine, Blue?'

The dog responded by licking his hand.

'That you, Clem?' a voice called out from inside the barn.

'Sure is, little brother,' came back the buoyant response. 'Where you hiding yourself? Still playing games, eh?' Although sad that his father was not there to greet him as well as Blue, Clem's mood lifted on hearing the welcome greeting from his young brother.

'I'm over here in the barn,' hollered Mace from his place of concealment. 'Come on over. I got some'n in here to show you.'

Clem's tanned features screwed up in bafflement. What was the little guy up to? Clem had been the butt of his young sibling's practical jokes in the past. Gingerly he approached the open barn.

He paused in the doorway and looked around. Everything appeared in order. Straw was piled up neatly to one side, saddles and horse tack were clean and well-cared for.

'Over here, Clem.' The raised voice came from the back of the barn behind a stall. 'You'll never believe what I've uncovered.'

Intrigued, the newcomer stepped inside and moved towards the sound of the still hidden voice. The squeal of a rusted chained wheel overhead drew his attention.

Only just in time.

Looking up, his bulging peepers saw a heavy wooden crate come tumbling down from the roof. Instinctively, Clem threw himself to one side. The box crashed to the ground inches from his body. Wooden splinters flew in all directions, one gouging a lump from his cheek. Otherwise he was untouched.

But the consequences, had he not been alerted, did not bear thinking about.

His well-planned scheme thwarted, Mace dashed out from the stall wielding a pitchfork. A hysterical scream of frustration issued from between clenched teeth as he lunged at the prone form of his hated sibling.

Although stunned from the shock of what he thought had been an accident, Clem's instinct for survival immediately kicked in.

His body twisted sideways. The deadly prongs jabbed into the earth floor beside his head.

'What in thunder's going on, yuh crazy kid?' yelled Clem, scrambling crablike away from this demonic fiend glaring down at him. 'That crate could have killed me. And now you're trying to finish the job.'

The only response he received was a garbled scream of rage as Mace Gifford discarded the fork and grabbed a Bowie knife from his belt. Another manic howl disgorged from the twisted maw as he charged at the object of his loathing.

There was no finesse, no deliberated skill in the attack. It was the action of a blood-crazed screwball whose mind had disintegrated.

Clem slewed to one side as the slashing knife flew past his head. He grabbed hold of Mace's swinging arm, holding it aloft. Together the brothers grappled for possession of the deadly blade. Teeth bared like those of an irate puma, eyes red-rimmed and bulging,

Mace wrestled his brother to the ground.

Over and over they rolled in the dust, each striving to gain the upper hand. No words were uttered. Death was only inches away as straining muscles fought for possession of the knife.

Mace was the attacker who sought only to destroy, whereas his brother merely wanted to remove the threat to his life. More than anything, however, he wanted answers. Why had his young brother turned into a deranged killer?

Strength and age eventually told on the frenzied kid, enabling Clem to throw his brother off. He scrambled to his feet and kicked the knife out of Mace's hand. Following up his sudden advantage, Clem aimed a couple of stiff jabs to Mace's jaw, effectively terminating the lethal bout.

But Clem was taking no unnecessary risks. Quickly he secured the overwrought kid with rope. Then he threw a bucket of water over the recumbent form to revive him.

Mace spluttered and gurgled, struggling to free himself. Then he vented his spleen in no uncertain terms. Cussing and damning his elder brother's good fortune, Mace was in no mood for explanations.

'Damn blasted Judas,' he railed. 'You allus was the golden boy. Not content with getting all the attention, you then had to poison Pa against me. Cheating me outa my inheritance. By rights this farm oughta been mine.'

Clem sighed. So that was what this was all about. He tried placating the recalcitrant youth. But the belligerent kid refused to see sense. Nevertheless, Clem continued trying to make his brother understand.

'That's what I'm here for,' he insisted while struggling to remain calm under the vitriolic onslaught. 'I don't want the durned farm. It's all your'n. I'm heading west down New Mexico way. The last thing I want is being tied up on a farm.'

'I don't believe you,' countered

Mace, eyes glittering with manic intensity. 'One day you'll be back. And with a bunch of lawyers in tow to claim your rights.' Mace spat on the ground. 'Well, that's what I think of you and your promises.'

Clem stared long and hard at the young tearaway before replying. His words were carefully chosen and delivered in measured tones.

'If that's what you think, then you'd best leave now.' Clem hauled out his brother's gun to ensure that no further attempts were made on his life, then he cut the ropes that were securing Mace. 'Get your things and skedaddle. You're a durned fool, Mace. A mule-headed jackass. You could have had it all. Now you're worth nought but a tinker's cuss.'

Mace uttered a raging cackle of derision. He was past caring.

'Don't worry,' he snarled. 'I'm going. But one day I'll get you for this . . . brother. Make no mistake.'

Then he scrambled to his feet and

headed for the farmhouse to collect his gear. Within a half-hour, Mace Gifford had disappeared over the northern horizon in a swirl of dust.

No further word had been exchanged between the two brothers. A melancholy aura hung over the Gifford place. A mood that no amount of whiskey could lighten. As Clem found to his cost the following morning.

A swift tour of inspection around the holding once his head had cleared revealed that young Mace had done his father proud. The Gifford farm was a going concern. But with a sub-zero interest in tilling the land, the remaining member of the family quickly sold up to the highest bidder. Then he made good his ambition to head West to the edge of the frontier and beyond.

Since that time Clem Gifford had heard nothing of or from his brother.

Until now.

5

Trinity Pass

The three fingers of orange sandstone standing in the middle of the mountain gap were instantly recognizable. Any religious significance attributed to this feature of Trinity Pass had been lost in the mists of time. Carved and shaped by centuries of windblown sand, the rock pinnacles now resembled a trio of gossiping harpies.

Clem secreted himself adjacent to the middle one. He settled down to await the hangman's arrival, built a fire and set the coffee pot bubbling. An hour passed before the steady clop of an approaching horse reached his ears. The trail wove a tortuous course between the three Trinities, passing near to Clem's camp.

The plotter stepped out and hailed

the newcomer with a breezy salutation.

'Howdy there, stranger,' he warbled, lifting a hand in greeting. A broad smile of welcome was pasted across his tanned visage. 'You're the first human I've laid eyes on in two weeks.'

'Is that a fact, sir?' came back an equally genial rejoinder.

'Sure is,' Clem continued sipping the mug of coffee clutched in his hand. 'Plenty of mangy critters around, but no proper company, if'n you catches my drift.' The guy nodded in agreement. 'Got myself lost searching after an illusory goldstrike some jasper told me about in Las Cruces. Maybe you'd oblige me by sharing this pot of excellent Arbuckle with a lonesome traveller like yourself.'

'That sure is a tempting offer,' said the portly hangman. 'But I'm in something of hurry.'

'Business calls, eh?' chortled Clem, glancing at the array of ropes strapped to the sides of the rider's mount.

'You could say that,' concurred the

florid dude, removing his beaverskin hat to reveal a bald pate. He extracted a silk handkerchief and carefully mopped away the beads of sweat bubbling on his dome. 'A heinous case of murder that needs attending to in Alamagordo in three days' time.'

Clem couldn't help noticing that the dude's attire was completely ill-suited to the arid terrain. The tight collar and necktie encasing a thick neck complemented the heavy serge of a black suit. All sober and businesslike ready for the forthcoming task.

The guy huffed and puffed, his red face oozing more sweat.

'Sure is a hot one,' he ventured. Hooking out a water bottle, he took a sip of the brackish liquid.

'Got me some prime cuts sizzling in the pan over yonder, and far too many fried potatoes for one man.' Clem took another drink of coffee, smacking his lips as he relished the strong flavour. 'Smells mighty good from where I'm standing.' He fixed a pleading eye on to the hovering ropeman. 'And with a family-sized tin of peaches for dessert cooling in that there spring, you'd be doing me a big favour. I just hate throwing good food away.'

'Well . . . ' The single word was drawled out as the guy hesitated. 'Maybe I could break my journey for a spell.' The hangman licked his thick lips while unconsciously patting his rotund girth. It was the thought of the cold peaches that had done the trick.

Clem suppressed a grin of satisfaction.

'Then step down, friend,' he invited, with an over-familiar spirit of geniality, 'and stretch your legs while enjoying one of Havana's finest.' He handed the guy a fat cigar and applied a scratched vesta.

The little guy drew in the smoke and sighed with contentment as he perched his ample rump down on a flat slab of rock. 'Seems like it was my lucky day you getting lost and all.'

'I'm the one who should be grateful

to you, sir,' Clem responded with vigour. He truly meant it, although his reasons were some somewhat different from those assumed by the visitor.

Time passed pleasantly enough.

The steaks were eaten with relish, the peaches drooled over. However, unbeknown to the innocent official, Clem had added a tot of whiskey to each mug of coffee supped. A potent ingredient which encouraged the neck-stretcher to open up.

His guest's tongue having been thoroughly loosened, Clem set to work extracting as much information as possible from the inebriated dude.

Thaddeus Wicklow was proud of his calling and considered himself to be at the peak of his profession. He was happy to expound on the finer points of the essential job he performed in bringing law and order to the territory.

With judicious encouragement from his host, Wicklow proceeded to clarify the deft touches needed to ensure that each despatch, as he called them, was done cleanly and efficiently. He also emphasized that it was important to ensure that the dignity of the 'client' was maintained right up to the final drop.

That meant taking great care to have the correct length of rope.

'Some fellows just don't care. No pride. All they want is to get the job done, collect their fee and drink it down in the nearest saloon.' The hangman shook his head in distaste. 'I tell you, sir, I've witnessed brutish fiascos where the client's head has been ripped clean off his shoulders. Messy, decidely messy.' His pudgy nose twitched. 'And certainly not the way that Thaddeus Wicklow does business.'

He paused to take another sip of the most excellent coffee, likewise relishing the second cigar of the day.

'A good hangman should always ensure that the neck is cleanly broken. And that means positioning the noose knot firmly behind the right ear.' At this point he struggled to his feet. Weaving a serpentine course, he tottered over to his horse. He extracted a rope with which he demonstrated the true art of the efficient 'despatch'.

Clem allowed the little guy to have his say without interruption. There was no denying that Wicklow was enthusiastic. To be sure, here was a guy who truly enjoyed his work. After staggering back to his seat, Wicklow imbibed another appreciative taste of the coffee.

'A fine brew you have here, Mister . . . erm, I didn't catch your name, sir?' he solicited. Bleary eyes battled to focus on his attentive host.

'Gi — ' Clem almost gave the game away. Even a greenhorn chock full to the gills with five-star whiskey would smell a rat if'n he gave his real monicker. 'Gilligan,' he said quickly, 'Mort Gilligan hailing from Fort Worth in Texas.'

'You're a long way from home, Mr Gilligan,' the swaying form said and hiccuped.

'About that clean break,' Clem

pressed the guy to continue with the vital aspects of his explanation.

He wanted to make absolutely certain that he had the technique well and truly mastered. There would doubtless be numerous officials present to witness the event. Any suspicions regarding the hangman's serious intentions to pervert the course of justice could well end with both brothers swinging in the breeze.

A double hanging that he was determined to avoid.

'Ah, yes, the final farewell.' Wicklow chuckled at his own witticism before expanding further on the procedure.

By the time that Thaddeus Wicklow had keeled over, snoring like a overfed boar — an apt description, mused Clem — the hunter had absorbed all the information he needed to make at least a spirited attempt at emulating the expected conduct of an official hangman.

This would also have been Wicklow's first visit to Alamagordo, which was a bonus. It meant that nobody would recognize him. The only downside was the fact that Wicklow's sombre attire did not fit Clem. He would need to acquire a fresh set of duds. It would not do for the official hangman to conduct his business in range gear.

That would entail a detour through Tularosa.

A coyote howled somewhere in the distance. It was time to move.

The sleeping Wicklow would be out for the count until well after dark. Too late to leave his enforced camp until the morning. Then it would take him three days' walking to reach the nearest trading post at Elephant Butte. By that time Clem intended to have freed his brother and to have disappeared into the fastnesses of the Sacramentos, back to his hideout.

He had no wish to harm his innocent guest. So he left behind a canteen of water and some sourdough biscuits. Enough to sustain the guy at least as far as Elephant Butte. That would give

Clem the chance to carry out the tricky business he had set himself.

After breaking camp he examined Wicklow's accoutrements — the ropes, leather straps, head bags and manacles. Then he mounted up and set off, leading the other guy's fully laden horse.

'*Adios, amigo*!' Clem tipped his hat to the recumbent form. 'You done me a big favour, Thaddeus. Perhaps I can to repay you some day.'

An owl hooted in agreement as he nudged the paint into a steady trot.

6

Man in Black

Two days later the unusual sight of a man in black, complete with silk derby perched on his head and leading a packhorse, jogged down the main street of Alamagordo.

Unlike most of the other towns he had passed through, this one had a distinctive Mexican feel to it. Adobe was the dominant building material.

The most recent erections, however, were of clapboard with signs proclaiming the wares on offer inside the various establishments. Some had adopted the American design feature of a squared-off false front with fancy carved crenellations.

Saloons with evocative names abounded. The Black Dog, Elkhorn and Blue Flamingo each proclaimed their business with garish signboards. But it was the Golden Nugget that stood out from the rest. One of the few brick buildings, it occupied a full block.

Wide sombreros mingled with the American Stetsons. It was clearly a town in transition.

Clem had changed into the unfamiliar garb when the town first came into view. As he passed people stopped what they were doing; pensive frowns were directed at the newcomer.

Everyone in town was aware of the gruesome event that was to take place the following day. Most were looking forward to the due process of the law, especially the after-hanging shindig being organized by the town council in the Golden Nugget.

Yet the appearance of the second most important participant brought home the grim reminder of what it was all about.

The upright figure stared ahead, looking neither to right nor left as he pointed his horse down the middle of the rutted thoroughfare. As he noticed the marshal's office, he wheeled the paint to a halt outside. The bogus executioner dismounted, flicked an imaginary speck of dust from his shoulders, then stepped on to the boardwalk and knocked on the heavy oak door.

'Come in,' a gruff voice replied. 'Door's off the latch.'

Clem stepped inside. His imperious gaze swept around the cluttered interior of the musty office. A Wanted dodger caught his attention. The glowering face of El Camaleon stared back at him. Pointing at the well-known depiction, he announced in suitably sententious tones practised over the last two days, 'You can take that down, Marshal. I will doubtless be attending the scoundrel's send-off in due course at Las Cruces.'

'Good day to you, Mr Wicklow,' the lawman greeted his expected visitor. 'I was getting rather worried that you wouldn't be here on time to erm . . . attend to my client.'

'An unforeseen delay when one of my horses threw a shoe coming over Trinity Pass.' Clem removed his frock-coat with an impressive flourish, folded it and laid the garment across a chair. 'Now perhaps if I could see the man in question so as to measure him up?'

The marshal greeted the request with a quizzical frown.

'The release of the trap, sir,' the hangman enlightened his starpacking colleague while brandishing a tape measure. 'Very important to have the correct length of rope in order to achieve the necessary result when he drops.'

Marshal Brewer gave the explanation a curt nod, intimating that he knew all along what was required. In truth, this was the lawman's first hanging and he didn't quite know what the correct procedure entailed. But he certainly didn't want to give that impression.

'Everything is ready for you, Mr Wicklow,' he asserted briskly. 'And we've made sure that the trap is in good working order.'

'I'm sure it is, Marshal,' agreed the pompous official, stroking his waxed moustache. 'But I always like to check everything personally. Just to make sure. You understand?'

Brewer shrugged.

'And now, the prisoner if you will?'

The marshal grabbed a bunch of keys and opened the door leading into the cell block. Only one of the three cells was occupied. Sprawled on a grubby cot, the sorry sight that met Clem's eyes brought a lump to his throat. This was the first time he had set eyes on his brother since that fateful day four years earlier.

Brewer unlocked the door. It swung open, squealing on rusted hinges that sounded like a trapped rodent. The recumbent form did not appear to have heard. Mace made no move even to turn his head.

'Visitor to see you, Gifford,' snapped the lawdog, taking a step back, hand firmly grasping the holstered Smith & Wesson revolver on his right hip. 'He's here to measure you up. And not for a new suit.' Brewer chortled at the joke as Clem moved forward into the confined space.

'If you could stand up, Mr Gifford, it would make my job a sight easier.'

It took all Clem's concentration to punch out the request in the authoritative tone of one in his position. He coughed to hide his anguish at seeing his only kin reduce to the shambling wreck now slumped before him.

There was still no response from the prisoner.

'Mr Gifford? If you please?' said Clem, nudging the supine body.

'Hangman's speaking to you, mister,' rasped Brewer. 'Best do as he says if'n you know what's good for you. A few extra bruises ain't gonna matter none at this stage in the game.'

Mace grunted, then levered himself up on to his feet.

'Thank you, sir,' came the croaked response from the bogus hangman. His eyes were fixed on to the bowed head of lank greasy hair. His whole being willed the owner to look up. 'I need you stand up straight, please.'

Slowly, the head rose.

Glassy eyes, devoid of any sign of life, fastened on to the visitor. But Mace failed to recognize his brother. Perhaps it was the moustache, the unexpected attire. Or maybe his mind had shut down. The ordinary, mundane aspects of life held no interest for a man condemned to die on the morrow. It could have been the Devil himself speaking. Mace Gifford was merely going through the motions, a man awaiting his destiny.

'Much obliged, Mace,' whispered the visitor, brandishing his tape measure. His words were uttered in his own distinctive mid-Western brogue. 'I need to make sure that you're good and ready for what's gonna happen in the morning.'

Something about that accent appeared to penetrate the fog of Mace Gifford's sluggish brain. And that face. He'd seen it before someplace.

'Everything is gonna be just fine, Mace,' intoned the figure in black, stressing each syllable. 'I'll be with you all the way.'

Both men locked eyes.

That was when Mace Gifford knew.

His mouth fell open. Then just as quickly, it closed as the realization slammed home that death at the end of a rope might possibly be averted. The already cadaverous features turned a ghostly white with the shock of such an unlikely encounter.

With the greatest effort, the condemned man forced his drawn features to remain blank and inscrutable. No sense alerting a suspicious jigger like Milton Brewer to the fact that all was not as it seemed.

And so the due process of law was conducted.

Once he had finished the charade, Clem moved back into the corridor allowing the marshal to lock the door.

A brisk nod. Then a half-smile passed

between the two brothers.

Mace Gifford was still in a state of shock. He could barely credit that he might now have a chance of thwarting the hangman's rope. The deception still had to be pulled off. But where nothing but gloom had enveloped the young tearaway's thoughts moments before, there was now a glimmer of hope.

More than a glimmer. The odds had definitely swung in his favour.

'I would like to examine the gallows personally if you have no objection, Marshal,' said Clem. He moved towards the back door of the cell block where it opened onto the enclosed execution yard. 'Just to make certain that everything is operating to my satisfaction.'

'Go ahead, Mr Wicklow,' replied the lawman. 'Want any assistance?'

'No thank you, sir,' came back the somewhat blunt retort. 'I prefer to do this alone. Thank you, all the same.'

Brewer shrugged and turned away to resume his work back in the office.

Clem stepped purposefully over to the grim structure, noting with a satisfied nod that the raised platform containing the trap was covered in at the front ensuring that nobody could witness the body in its final death throes. Far more important, it would hide the fact that the said body was still very much in the land of the living.

Moving catlike around the side of the platform, he examined the inner sanctum. At the rear was a door through which the bodies of victims were removed for burial. Like most other towns, the cemetery included a section reserved for those who had met a violent end. They became known universally as Boot Hill, the first such place being in Dodge City, Kansas.

The door was yet another feature that Clem intended taking advantage of.

Yes indeed, he mused, once again surveying the death-dealing contraption from the front. The officially sanctioned construction had played right into his hands. A loose smile softened the tightness of his face as he returned to the office.

'Everything to your liking?' enquired the lawman looking up from his accounts ledger.

'It most certainly is,' averred the hangman. 'Couldn't be better.' The smile was genuine, but for a different reason from that assumed by Milton Brewer. 'I will see you first thing on the morrow, sir,' he announced setting his hat straight. 'An early night for me.'

And with that jaunty remark, he left the law office. A black cat sauntered across the street in his path. Was that a good omen? Certainly not for the town of Alamagordo, he hoped, crossing his fingers. A little superstition didn't go amiss in such circumstances.

There was still a couple of hours of daylight left. Time enough to enjoy a good meal before arranging a rapid departure once the charade had been enacted.

He wandered down the street. Light spilled from the open door of the Glad

Tidings diner. Clem peered through the front window.

The woman bustling between the tables caught his eye. Although an elegant sashaying was more of an apt description for Marcia Tripp, the proprietor. Thick auburn tresses tied back with a green ribbon complementing the hourglass figure encased in a green-and-white gingham dress gave her a rustic, somewhat hayseed appeal. Maybe it was an image she sought to create in order to draw in the customers.

It certainly appeared to be working.

The vast majority of the patrons were men, whose eyes appeared to be fixed more on the smoothly flowing contours of the woman than their food.

Clem could readily understand their fixation. Marcia Trip was without doubt a handsome female.

The arrival of the man in black attracted a host of turned heads. Everybody in town recognized the top hat and cut of his attire. But it was the piercing blue eyes that drew Marcia Tripp's gaze. They seemed to reach deep within her very being. A tremble rippled through her voluptuous frame as she approached the hangman.

'Table for one, mister?'

The enquiry emerged more as a hoarse croak.

'If you please, madam.' The entrancing stranger gave her a graceful bow as she ushered him to a table over in the corner of the busy restaurant.

'Today's special is steak and onion pie,' she said, unable to drag her eyes away from the mesmeric allure of the man's gaze. Was it the macabre choice of occupation he pursued, or something deeper? He certainly wasn't how she had expected a hangman to look.

'Made by your own fair hand, I trust?'

A nod was all Marcia could manage.

'Seems good to me,' replied the smiling diner who was equally smitten with this vision in gingham. 'And a side order of cornbread would help it slip down a treat.'

The rest of the evening passed without any further communication between server and serviced. Yet both knew that something had happened that neither could quite pin down.

Only later, when Clem was paying his bill, did he deign to make a forward suggestion that would enable their fleeting contact to be resumed at some point. When that would be, the bogus hangman could not say, in view of the circumstances surrounding his sudden appearance in Alamagordo. But he could not help himself.

'Perhaps when my business in Alamagordo is completed,' he proposed tentatively, 'you could be persuaded to take a buggy ride so that we might become better acquainted?'

The entreaty hung in the air while the lady considered the suggestion. She tilted her head in thought, a long tapering finger tapping her chin.

'Perhaps.'

Clem had to be satisfied with that as Marcia sauntered away. A wry smile below her arched eyebrows told him, however, all that he needed to know.

But whether that assignation would ever take place was in the lap of the gods.

7

Vanishing Act

Clem was already awake when a natural alarm clock in the form of a rooster's call pierced the dawn silence. Sleep had not come easily. A series of disturbing dreams had brought him instantly awake, sweat pouring down his face. All of them involved a rope tightening around his neck. He was, therefore, more than glad of the watery light of the dawn filtering through the thin curtain of his window.

He dressed quickly in the unfamilar clothes. A splash of water on his face dispersed the macabre images of night. Then he hurried down the back stairs to ensure that the two horses were ready at the back of the jailhouse yard. Now that the time had almost arrived, Clem felt invigorated, ready and eager for the bizzarre role he had to play.

The hanging was to be an early affair.

Tradition dictated that the condemned man should be dead and buried before the ninth hour. In the case of Mace Gifford, the ruling had been amended to enable the body to be laid out in the undertaker's window for all to witness.

There was nothing so mesmeric as the viewing of a corpse following an official despatch. With hangings now being performed in sequestration, this was the next best option. The council was expecting a large influx of voyeurs, all of whom would be spending money in Alamagordo's wide range of saloons and emporia.

After adjusting his necktie and smoothing down the creases in his black suit, Clem Gifford — alias Thaddeus Wicklow, territiorial hangman — squared his shoulders and entered the marshal's office.

Numerous officials were awaiting him. Included in the august reception party were members of the town council, the undertaker and the preacher. The last of these was nervously clutching his Bible. Also present was the editor of the *Alamagordo Journal* to record the occasion in all its lurid detail. It would be front-page news the next day.

And then of course there was the doctor.

The latter's presence was the only fly in the ointment. He would be required immediately after the event to officially pronounce that the due process of law had been carried out and the felon was now deceased.

All night Clem had been figuring out how best to deal with this vexatious problem. For as soon as the medic saw the supposedly hanged man, he would know the truth. There was only one course of action left open to him. The medic would have to be put out of action the moment he stepped behind the hidden barrier under the gallows.

'Good day to you, Mr Wicklow,'

greeted the marshal. A sardonic salutation in view of the circumstances. 'Could I introduce you to the officials who are required to be present at the erm . . . event.'

Hands were quickly shaken, names announced, all of which Clem instantly forgot.

He drew in a deep breath.

'Well, gentlemen,' he asserted briskly. The queasy fluttering in his stomach was forcibly subdued as he continued, 'we need to get this business over and completed lickety-split. Both for our sakes and that of our client.' Clem eyed them all in turn. His probing gaze was avoided. 'Any questions before we begin?'

Shuffling feet and downcast expressions were the sole response to the hangman's query.

This was not a civic occasion to which the members of the town council had been looking forward. It would leave a nasty taste in the mouth. Much more to their liking was the social gathering to follow in the Golden Nugget. In consequence, they were eager to get the business over with as quickly as possible.

It was the general view that adding the screen to conceal the actual moment of death had been a good idea. The last thing anybody wanted was to be seen vomiting up their breakfast.

'Then please make your way into the yard through the side gate so as not to cause any alarm to the prisoner. From cell to gallows, the whole business should be complete within three minutes.' The hangman coughed out a forced laugh as he declared proudly, 'My record is two minutes and thirty-five seconds. Perhaps we can beat that today.'

Accompanied by the marshal and his deputy on each side, the prisoner with hands bound behind his back was quickly hustled into the yard. Clem followed behind. The officials were lined up. Some were looking decidedly green about the gills.

Once positioned on the trap atop the platform, Clem took over.

He placed the hood over the condemned man's head. Then he positioned the noose correctly. Unfortunately, no opportunity was afforded to whisper any last-minute instruction to his brother. For on his right stood the preacher reading the Bible in a suitably dolorous voice.

Time hung heavy over the macabre gathering.

All eyes focused on the marshal. A brief nod and the trap lever was pulled. A lone coyote out on the flats howled in sympathy.

An ominous bang sliced through the chilly atmosphere as the heavy trapdoor struck a beam beneath. Instantly, the condemned man disappeared from view amidst an audible gasp from the assembled dignitaries.

Straight away Clem descended the steps and disappeared behind the wooden screen. His brother had landed on a bed of straw placed there the night before to ease his fall. The rope was still around his neck, its extra length preventing the requisite neck break.

'Don't move!' hissed Clem through clenched teeth as he slit the cords binding his brother's hands. 'The doc's coming.'

'You said something, Mr Wicklow?' enquired the medic as he stepped into the gloomy confines below the gallows.

'Just mumbling to myself is all, Doc,' replied Clem, allowing the medic to move forward to examine the expected corpse. 'Everything appears to have gone to plan.'

As the doctor passed by to take a look at the prone form, Clem leaned forward and struck him on the back of the neck with the stiffened side of his hand. It was a manoeuvre he had learned from the owner of a Chinese laundry whose murdered son he had once avenged.

He had called it kung fu. But too much force and the blow could kill a man. Clem administered just sufficient power merely to knock the guy out. The doctor fell to the ground without uttering a sound and was quickly bound hand and foot.

'Sorry about that, Doc,' muttered Clem. Then to his brother, 'Let's get outa here, pronto,' he urged dragging his trembling brother to his feet. 'We ain't got more'n a couple of minutes to escape before the marshal becomes suspicious.'

Mace Gifford's legs felt like jelly. He could barely stand, such had been the grimness of his ordeal. He was sweating buckets. His mouth hung open as he gulped air into tortured lungs. Right until the very last minute he had been convinced that something would go wrong. Even now, he could barely credit that freedom was within his reach.

Only when he tumbled on to the straw and realized that he was still alive did the notion infiltrate Mace Gifford's torpid brain that he might actually have escaped the hangman's noose.

But they still had to get away. Mace allowed his brother to half-carry, half-drag him out through the back door. Somehow, he was bungled on to a horse.

'Dig in with them spurs,' exhorted Clem, slapping his brother's mount on the rump, 'if'n you want to see tomorrow's dawn.'

With a drumming of galloping hoofs the two horses took off, vanishing in the early morning shadows. Twisting and turning through a series of narrow alleys, Clem headed south-east, keeping the golden orb of the rising sun all the while on his left hand.

Within minutes they burst out of the constricting limits of the town's back alleys. Neither looked back, but urged their mounts onward at a frenetic gallop. So far luck had been on their side. No sounds of pursuit reached Clem's ears, although by this time the authorities must surely have got wise to the fact that their loudly trumpeted hanging had been so ignominiously subverted.

The agent of that bungle couldn't resist a brief smile of satisfaction. Playing the part of a pompous hangman had proved to be an exhilarating deception. And the release of his brother couldn't have gone down better, so to speak.

However, they still had to get away unscathed.

Clem had no doubts that a heavily armed posse would be quickly despatched in pursuit of the fugitives. Such a humiliating act performed right under the noses of the town dignitaries would have left all concerned with red faces and eager for revenge.

So it was important that the direction of their escape remained a secret.

Elation at having successfully carried off the reckless ploy was quickly supplanted by a mood of grim determination. It was now imperative to put the greatest possible distance between the fugitives and the town's fuming administrators.

Clem's destination was a hideout discovered deep within the fastness of the Sacramento Mountains. From there he had planned and executed all his bounty-hunting exploits in this part of the New Mexico territory.

* * *

Throughout the day, Clem led his brother up a sequence of narrow winding deer trails amidst the dense blanket of ponderosa pine that formed the Lincoln Forest. Not until they had emerged above the treeline did he deem it safe to call a halt for the day.

Late-afternoon shadows played across the austere landscape blurring the tones of orange, green and brown to a murky ochre. Circling buzzards drifted on the warm thermals overhead, eyeing these intruders from afar. A squirrel paused halfway up a tree, the bushy red of its tail starkly contrasted against the dark trunk.

Little had been said during the

protracted journey. Only when they had settled down for the night over mugs of coffee was the full explanation of Mace Gifford's shady past and eventual incarceration in the Alamagordo jail revealed. Once started, the floodgates had opened.

Clem likewise apprised his brother of his own dubious exploits. The most startling of these was his revelation that he was none other than the notorious bounty hunter known as Montero.

Such was the elation of the two brothers at meeting up again under such bizarre circumstances that the original cause of their split was forgotten.

'You have to believe me, Clem,' Mace averred forcefully for the umpteenth time. 'I was set up. Sure, that gutless cardsharp had been cheating. And I threatened to get even with him. But it wasn't me that pulled the trigger. That's the gospel truth. It was those two letters written in the dust that sealed my fate.' He slammed a balled fist into the palm of his hand in frustration. 'There has to be somebody else in that durned town whose name begins with MA. Find him and that's gotta be the killer.'

Beseeching eyes silently implored his brother to accept the anguished plea of innocence. Clem pulled on his cheroot. Spiralling tendrils of smoke drifted in the still air.

Before he had time to voice an opinion, an alien sound grated on their ears. It was a dry twig breaking. It came sharp and distinct in the thinning mountain air. And it had come from the cluster of trees backing on to a wedge of fractured sandstone cliff some hundred yards distant.

Probably a woodland creature on the move, Clem surmised. Perhaps a porcupine or cottontail rabbit. But he was taking no chances.

8

Unexpected Visitor

'Make like you're alone and getting ready to bed down,' Clem whispered. He drew his pistol and moved silently over to conceal himself behind a clump of juniper. 'If'n it's a bushwhacker I'll grab the critter when he steps into the open.'

He didn't have long to wait.

A figure gingerly emerged from the tree cover leading a horse no more than ten feet from where Clem was hiding. The wide-brimmed hat concealed the intruder's face. Giving the varmint no chance to ambush his brother, Clem stepped behind and wrestled the possible dry-gulcher to the ground.

For a skulking thief the guy put up little resistance. In fact, he seemed decidely lightweight, more akin to a sack of feathers. The truth was soon revealed when the intruder's hat was knocked off and a high-pitched yelp of surprise emanated from his startled face.

Clem stepped back, gaping at the smoothly aquiline features of none other than . . . a young woman.

He quickly hauled the stunned newcomer to her feet.

'Who in thunderation are you?' came the startled question from an equally bewildered Clem Gifford. 'And why are you trailing us?'

'Ellie!'

The blunt exclamation from Mace brought his brother up short.

'You know this gal, boy?' snapped Clem whose normally cool demeanour was being sorely stretched. 'If so, then I figure some kinda explanation is due.' He peered at both parties from beneath beetled brows. 'From both of you.'

Mace ignored his brother's insistent demand. He rushed over to the girl and took her in his arms. For the first time they were able to hold each other close without the cold hardness of prison bars between them. It was a tender if brief moment.

Clem turned away feeling rather awkward in the presence of such an emotional reunion. This was something for which he had not bargained.

It was Mace who broke the spell, realizing that there was indeed an explanation due. He had not mentioned his unlikely affair with the reluctant calico queen, figuring it to be just a fleeting moment that was past and gone. No way was he ever going to see the girl again following the escape.

Yet here she was, wrapped in his arms. A dream come true.

'This is my long-lost brother, Clem,' he said as they reluctantly drew apart. 'We had a falling out some years ago. But he heard about my predicament and came a-calling. And it's sure lucky for me that he didn't hold no grudges.'

Addressing his brother, Mace then introduced the newcomer. 'This here lovely creature is Ellie Spavin,' he said proudly. 'She's the only person in Alamagordo who didn't believe I killed that gambler.'

Clem uttered the obvious query.

'So how come you managed to trail us all the way from town?' He fixed the girl with a probing regard. 'Strikes me that if'n you could follow us without being spotted, then like as not those angry hornets that we reckoned to have hoodwinked will also be hot on our heels.'

Ellie had an immediate answer. She took a sip of the welcome coffee that Clem handed to her before elucidating.

'My pa was an army scout for William Fetterman when the Bozeman Trail was first opened back in '62. He moved south only days before the captain and eighty of his men were massacred by Crazy Horse. You heard about it?'

Clem nodded. He had been around that neck of the woods when Red Cloud was threatening to wipe out the thinly spread troops. 'As I recall, a peace was struck in '78 at Laramie.'

'Well, he taught me all the rudiments of good tracking from a young age. I was a real tomboy in those days.' Her bright laugh was infectious. The two men joined in.

'You sure as heck have changed,' said Mace with a sigh. His eyes rolled; he was mesmerised by this winsome creature.

Ellie cocked her head, acknowledging the doting compliment before continuing, 'Pa sure would have been proud of me. Only mistake I've ever made was that broken twig.' Her comely features suggested a self-mocking rebuke. 'It was seeing Mace by the fire. I couldn't wait to surprise him. But don't you guys fret none. That posse has no idea you've headed south-east into the Sacramentos.'

Clem accepted the girl's explanation. But he was still somewhat fazed by the idea that he would now have to nursemaid a woman.

Ellie appeared to read his thoughts.

'Seeing as how I know that Mace is innocent,' she said, 'I figured you'd be wanting to uncover the real killer.'

'That's the general idea,' agreed Clem. 'Although I ain't too sure how to set about it.'

'Well, that's where I can help out.'

Raised eyebrows from both men encouraged the girl to continue.

'Marcia Tripp, who runs the hash house in town doesn't need me to start serving tables for another two weeks. That's when her current help leaves to have a baby. That means I can go back and sniff around some while you guys camp out in the hills close to town.'

The suggestion received a tight-lipped scowl of scepticism from Clem Gifford.

'I ain't sure about that, Ellie,' he muttered, concern for the girl's safety written across his features.

'Why not?' the girl hurried on undaunted. 'It'll be easy as falling off a log for me to slip out of town and fill you in with what I've learned. And when the posse comes back empty handed, the marshal's bound to figure you've left the territory for good.'

Mace was far more positive.

'I reckon its a dandy plan' he enthused, eyes afire with fresh hope of clearing his name. 'What d'yuh say then, Clem? Ellie sure ain't just a purty face, is she?'

Clem shrugged. His features relaxed. It was true that the girl's scheme had a great deal of merit. A slow grin replaced the louring grimace of disapproval.

'Glad to see that someone's finally gonna take you in hand.' He threw a grin at his brother. 'And as for Ellie's plan —' His lean features assumed a more sombre cast as he addressed the pair of cooing lovebirds. '— it sounds good to me. Although I don't want you putting yourself in any danger, Ellie. You'll need to be mighty careful to avoid raising any suspicions. The authorities will know how you feel about Mace here having scarpered and they'll be watching you like a hawk.'

The younger Gifford responded with a vigorous nod of agreement. Tenderly he squeezed the girl's tiny hand.

'You sure this is what you want to do, Ellie?' he pressed. 'Now that I've found you, no way am I gonna put your life at risk even if it is to prove my innocence.'

'Listen up, mister,' rapped the spirited young filly. 'If'n we're to make a go of things then it's gonna be on the right side of the law. I want to settle down and raise a family in peace. Not to be forever awaiting the arrival of some bounty hunter to call you out.'

A poignant look passed between the two brothers.

'Is it some'n I said?' Ellie frowned.

'Ever heard of a guy going by the name of Montero?' asked Mace.

'Who hasn't?' answered the girl. 'They say that varmint has gotten more notches on his gun than Doc Holliday.'

'Don't believe everything you read in the papers, miss,' replied Clem, his expression breaking into a loose smile.

Ellie shot him a quizzical look, then gasped aloud. You mean . . . ?' She was lost for words.

'He sure is,' Mace affirmed proudly. 'It was the great Montero himself that busted me outa jail and left them knuckleheads waiting around like Thanksgiving turkeys.' He howled with laughter at Ellie's stunned expression.

'N-no offence, I didn't mean nothing . . . ' stammered the overwhelmed girl.

'None taken.' Clem grinned back. 'And I agree with Mace. Any suspicions fall on your shoulders, then back off.'

* * *

Around noon of the following day Clem indicated a narrow rift branching off the main valley.

'The hideout is tucked away out of sight in Tomahawk Canyon,' he explained. 'There's only one way in and out. So we need to ensure there are no stray hoofprints around the entrance that will give us away. Not that I'm expecting any visitors. This place is well off the main trails. The only jaspers passing this way are likely to be prospectors and guys on the dodge.'

He nudged his brother with an elbow.

'Don't worry, Mace,' murmured Clem, placating the other's waspish grunt. 'I ain't gonna deliver you up for the reward that's certain to be put out.'

'You sure ain't, mister,' asserted Ellie firmly. 'Only person that's hauling in this fella is me.' The girl stood her ground, hands clamped to her slim hips. She cast the brothers a challenging regard that any man would ignore at his peril.

'So that's me told good and proper,' replied Clem, tipping his hat in acknowledgement. Then with a pensive twist of the lip, he added, 'What I've only just cottoned to is that I'm now gonna be decorating a dodger as well.'

'Seems like I'm the only one in the clear.' Ellie chuckled. 'Maybe it oughta be me doing all the collecting.'

That declaration brought an outburst of hearty laughter from all three fugitives as they jigged their mounts towards the narrow entrance to Tomahawk Canyon. A little later they emerged from a circle of trees into a clearing hemmed in by a towering ring of protective cliffs.

A log cabin had been erected at the far side of what had once been a thriving miners' camp.

'I came upon this place by accident,' Clem explained. 'The mother lode must have been worked out and the place abandoned. But it sure makes an ideal hideout.' A more circumspect remark followed. 'Best we let the dust settle for a few days before venturing back into the hornet's nest. I always keep a good stock of dry goods in case I need to rest up for a spell.'

9

The Chameleon Strikes

Around the same time that the fugitive trio were settling down in Tomahawk Canyon, events were about to blow up in Las Cruces.

'A visitor for you, Chameleon,' announced Sheriff Phelps. 'And a right purty one at that.'

A lascivious eye followed the sashaying hips of a buxom woman who stepped into the cell block. She was certainly well upholstered, just the way Morgan Phelps liked his women.

Expertly he frisked the visitor, allowing his hands to linger in certain prominent spots.

The woman wore her large plumed hat pulled low, keeping her face in shadow. Although it wasn't the woman's face that Phelps was bothered about. Her head was bent modestly forward as she reluctantly permitted herself to suffer the lawdog's inept fumbling.

She never uttered a word of complaint, which was understandable. The prisoner had informed Phelps that his visitor had been dumb from birth. Not a word had passed her lips since then.

'Best type of woman there is,' the sheriff had remarked on receiving the news. 'Keeps 'em from givin' a fella earache.'

'You sure are right there, Sheriff,' agreed the condemned felon. 'A man should be master of his own house.'

Satisfied, in more ways than one, Phelps motioned the visitor to enter the passage, where he opened the cell door.

'You have five minutes,' he said with a sneer, leaning his shoulder against the wall. 'Best make the most of it.'

'Surely you will allow me a private moment with my *novia*,' warbled the prisoner. Round eyes appealed to the lawman's more sympathetic side, if he had one. 'This may be the last time we can be alone before . . . ' He left the sentence unfinished.

The outcome of the trial of El Camaleon had been a foregone conclusion. And the territorial neck-stretcher was due in a couple of days to conclude the proceedings in time-honoured fashion. This time with an escort. Thaddeus Wicklow was taking no chances.

Phelps grunted, then levered himself off the wall.

'I'm keepin' the door open,' he said, 'So keep any shenanigans quiet. I don't want any sordid business disturbin' my dinner.'

Once out of sight, the two people quickly got down to 'business'. But not in the way that the sheriff expected. The prisoner placed a finger against his lips. Chaquita Esteban was none other than his sister. And a particularly verbose one at that. The last thing he needed now was for her to start chastizing him aloud.

That would surely alert the hovering

lawman that some chicanery was afoot.

The girl had been apprised of her brother's plan on a previous visit. Quickly she divested herself of the bulky dress, hat and long blonde wig. Manuel Esteban did likewise. Then they each donned the other's clothing.

El Camaleon was about to pull off the most audacious deception of his career.

Chaquita's pert nose wrinkled in disgust. Her brother clearly had not washed or been able to change his duds in a coon's age.

Next, the prisoner tied his sister up with some strips of blanket from his bunk. That way she could claim to have been attacked and left comatose on the bed. The girl had been reluctant when Manuel first outlined the plan. But he had assured his sister that no blame for the proposed escape would fall on her shoulders if she carried out his instructions to the letter.

Blood is thicker than water and Manuel was nothing if not persuasive.

And so she had finally agreed. The notion to play dumb had been Chaquita's. A stroke of pure genius according to her brother, that would certainly clinch the charade.

To lend authenticity to the subterfuge, Manuel had shaved off his moustache. A liberal dousing from Chaquita's scent bottle effectively removed the rank body odour that would have spoiled the illusion. And the wig fitted him perfectly. The wide-brimmed hat with its feathered accessory would also keep his face in shadow.

Only a close look would reveal the truth. For Morgan Phelps would be expecting a woman to emerge from the cell block.

The transformation was completed in less than five minutes.

A swift inspection of her brother by Chaquita, and he was ready once again to play the Chameleon. But this time it would be a rendezvous with the hangman if he failed.

★ ★ ★

Exhibiting an unaccustomed tenderness, Esteban the notorious killer laid the bound and gagged woman on the dirty bunk and covered her with a blanket. A peck on the cheek, then he called out to the waiting lawman.

'We are finished in here, Sheriff. My sister is ready to leave.'

A scraping chair sounded in the outer office. Esteban held his breath. The moment of truth had arrived.

As the lawman entered the cell block, the trickster turned his head away, ostensibly to give a last minute kiss to the person lying on the bunk. A key grated in the lock as the cell door opened.

The figure lying on the bunk did not move, Chaquita's face was hidden from view beneath the grubby blanket.

'Step outside, miss,' said Phelps, his gun drawn just in case the prisoner tried to escape. 'You got one more visit before the hangman does his work.'

Head bent low, her right hand clutching a lace handkerchief to her face to offer the illusion that she was crying, the 'woman' hurried out of the cell block.

'You want to join me in a cup of coffee, miss?' Phelps shouted after her disappearing back. But the object of his attention was already through the front door and striding down the boardwalk to the next block, where a horse had been left waiting.

Phelps uttered a derisive grunt.

'That woman of your'n seems to have taken this business to heart,' he scoffed at the covered figure on the bunk. He slammed the cell door shut. 'Don't know why. A scumbag like you deserves all that's coming to him.'

He aimed a globule of phlegm at the prisoner before returning to the accounts he was checking back in the office.

It would be noon before he discovered the startling truth.

El Camaleon made good his escape

from Las Cruces. Once clear of the town he discarded the female garb and changed into the spare clothes that Chaquita had packed in the saddlebags. More important, however, was the six-gun and shellbelt. It was unfortunately not one of the latest Colt revolvers. But the army Remington would serve its purpose until such time as he could regain his .45 from that gringo bounty hunter.

A mirthless smile creased the face of the fugitive when he recalled the reaction of Montero when his prisoner had first been incarcerated. The critter had been unaware that his shocked expression on learning the identity of the felon due to be hanged at Alamagordo had not gone unnoticed by El Camaleon.

At the time Manuel Esteban was too distraught at having been captured to pay it much heed. Only later when he had had time to think did the incident assume any significance.

The bounty hunter clearly knew the

condemned man. Not only that, he must be closely associated with the guy. On further reflection, Esteban had arrived at the conclusion that they must be related. In wanting to keep the knowledge secret, it was obvious that Montero intended to bust the guy out of jail.

So Alamagordo was now the destination of El Camaleon.

If his suspicions were correct, the gringo and his sidekick would have hightailed it by this time. But where would they have gone?

There was only one *hombre* who would likely have that sort of information. Eli Penrose stored up a lot more than just the goods on sale over the counter of his trading post. It was all tucked away inside that devious brain. So long as a questioner had the wherewithal to purchase information, Penrose generally had the answers.

Esteban cracked a hideous grimace.

Now there was another *bastardo* against whom the fugitive sought revenge. Now he could kill two birds with one stone. The operative word being 'kill'. It would only need a short detour to reach the Cabrio Trading Post.

* * *

The lonely outpost appeared to be devoid of customers. No horses were tethered outside, only the inevitable cluster of goats foraging in the rubbish heap at the side. Esteban gave a nod of satisfaction. There would just be the two of them. No witnesses to make life more complicated.

He dismounted some distance from the cabin and approached from an angle, to avoid being spotted by the shifty proprietor. After checking the load of his pistol the outlaw decided to adopt the strategy of his nemesis, Montero.

Circling behind the main structure, he slipped in through the back door. Although he was of a bulky build

Esteban was surprisingly nimble when the need arose. He paused inside the gloomy back room to listen for any signs as to the whereabouts of his quarry.

A shuffling of boxes in the main store told him that Penrose was at home and unaware of his presence. A dog barked somewhere outside. Esteban froze. The movement of goods on the far side of the door continued. Silently, Esteban opened the door and peered through.

There was Penrose, bent over a carton, examining the contents, completely oblivious of the approaching threat to his continued existence.

'Just like old times, Eli.'

The stark comment sliced through the fetid atmosphere as the newcomer reached for a bottle of hooch. Gripping the cork with his teeth, Esteban tugged it, spat it out and imbibed a generous slug.

Penrose dropped the carton and swung around. His face assumed a waxy pallor when he recognized the speaker.

'Y-you!' the trader gulped. 'H-how c-come . . . ?'

The outlaw ignored the stuttering reaction to his sudden and unexpected appearance. Casually he selected a cigar from the humidor on the counter and lit up. He nodded his approval.

'Here we are,' smirked the ghost from the past. 'You skulking in your midden, and me taking a drink while telling you about my latest exploits.' He puffed on the cigar before continuing, allowing the trader to sweat. 'Just like old times. Only difference now, *amigo*, is that you know what happened already, don't you?'

The lilting cadence had hardened to a blunt challenge.

'I . . . it wasn't my fault . . . ' spluttered the alarmed storekeeper backing away from this apparition who, he had figured, was swinging high on a gallows by now.

A display of mocking solemnity followed as the Mexican shook his head. His tongue clicked with a sneering trace of regret.

'You should not have sold out on me, Eli,' he said quietly. 'That was a foolish thing to do. One that could get you killed.' Even as he uttered the fateful words, the revolver had leapt into his hand. It swayed in front of the quaking Judas like an angry sidewinder.

'That durned bounty hunter forced me to — '

The waving gun cut short the impassioned plea of innocence.

'Save your shallow denials,' spat the scowling outlaw. 'I know exactly what happened. You thought to make money out of the situation by coming to a deal with the bounty hunter. That was a bad mistake.'

The hammer of the revolver snapped back to half-cock. It was a harsh click that heralded oblivion. Penrose's heart raced. More sweat bubbled across the bony face.

'But there is one way to save that miserable hide of your'n.'

'Anything, old buddy,' gasped out the

pitiful trader, grasping at straws. 'Just say the word and I'll do it.'

The Mexican responded with a shrivelling glower. The barrel of the Remington seemed like a cannon to the trembling trader.

'You are a man with much knowledge trapped inside here, *si*?' The gunman tapped the side of his head. 'Information that might come in useful to those with the money to pay for it.'

Penrose reacted with a look of puzzlement. 'I keep my ear to the ground if'n that's what you mean,' he said carefully.

'That is what I figured,' replied Esteban. 'So where do you suppose that Montero would go to hide out for a spell? Your life in exchange for that one small favour.'

Penrose was more than willing to pass the word in exchange for his life. He hurriedly blurted out what the bounty hunter had unwittingly disclosed.

'He hangs out in a place called

Tomahawk Canyon in the Sacramentos.'

'*Bueno, bueno*,' sang out the Mexican. 'That is all I wanted to know.'

A mirthless smile crossed his swarthy features. Any hope that Penrose had harboured about stepping back from the brink dissolved as the gun snapped to full cock.

'Y-you said I could go free for that piece of info.'

Esteban shook his head sorrowfully.

'I lied.'

The gun exploded. Two bullets struck the trader in the chest, slamming him back against the counter. His eyes rolled as the killer ambled over, the smoking pistol held down by his side.

'You should never have betrayed me, *amigo*. Such a double-dealing act deserves only one response.' A macabre grin played over the killer's features. A glassy eye peered up at him as the trader slid to the floor. The gun rose again. Another bullet spat from the barrel, burying itself in the victim's skull.

'One bird down, another to go.'

As he was leaving the store, Esteban grabbed one of the latest Winchesters from a rack behind the bar. A revolver was OK for close shooting, but a carbine was essential for middle-distance accuracy. Not as good as a Sharps or Whitney for long range, but a repeater would always have the edge.

10

Lucky Break

Immediately upon arriving back in Alamagordo, Ellie Spavin was arrested by the town marshal. She was accused of being an accomplice of the bogus hangman who had so successfully engineered the release of her lover. However, no proof could be unearthed that linked her with the cunning escapade. Following a somewhat heavy-handed grilling, Milton Brewer had been obliged to release the girl from custody.

Over the next week Ellie had made little progress in her search for the real killer of Honest Luke Torrance. Many of the townsfolk were suspicious of the ex-harlot. Her association with the escaped man, however brief, had not helped. People were loath to discuss the incident.

More serious was the occasion when she was heading back to her room above the Glad Tidings diner. Marcia Tripp was the one person in the town who had displayed any sympathy towards the girl. Ellie was due to start work in two days' time. It was fortunate that the job came with full board.

Her room was at the rear of the diner on the first floor. Access was by way of a narrow passage between the butcher's and a hardware store. After climbing the back stairs she entered the upper corridor. Her thoughts were wholly concentrated on the perplexing dilemma that was facing her. How was she going to discover who had killed the gambler?

Consequently she failed to notice that the lock on her door had been broken. She pushed it open and walked in, only to find a man sprawled on the bed. It was Charlie Boggs, a leery grin spread across his face. The door slammed shut as Biff Ryker emerged from behind it.

'Now maybe we can complete that

unfinished business your damn blasted hero spoilt before he escaped from jail,' Ryker spat, shucking off his jacket.

His partner immediately leapt off the bed and grabbed hold of the girl. He fastened a grubby hand over her mouth to prevent any screams for help. Rank lust oozing from every pore, both men urgently pulled at Ellie's clothing, eager to assuage their salacious hunger.

However, the girl was no pushover. She had toughened up since their previous encounter. Struggling like a wildcat, she lashed out with both feet. One boot caught Boggs on the leg. He grunted. But little damaged was done. However, during the frenzied defence of her dignity, a flailing leg slammed against an upright mirror. It crashed against a spindly table on which stood a large washbowl and jug.

The whole caboodle collapsed on to the floor. The mirror glass shattered amidst the broken crockery, spilling water across the bare floor boards.

So aroused were the two attackers on

seeing a bare breast hanging loose from Ellie's torn dress that they totally ignored the noise. Not so the proprietor and her dishwasher, who were engaged in their culinary duties immediately below Ellie's room.

After grabbing hold of suitable weaponry, they both scurried up the back steps and burst into the upper room. Abel Sankey held an old Manhattan .31. A large though reliable pistol, it looked like a cannon in the little guy's hand. Marcia Tripp had a meat cleaver raised above her thick auburn tresses.

'Leave her be!' growled the buxom café-owner.

'And keep your mitts away from them hoglegs else I'll ventilate your mangy hides,' added Sankey jabbing the pistol.

Suddenly confronted, the two assailants hastily buttoned themselves up. Ellie likewise hauled the bed cover across her exposed body.

'Seems like we got here just in time,'

snarled the incensed café-owner. The lethal blade of the cleaver glinted in the dim candlelight.

'They hurt you, honey?' enquired the girl's concerned employer.

Ellie was too stunned to utter a reply, merely shaking her head.

'That don't excuse the vile treatment you pair of horned toads were gonna mete out.' A savage smirk crossed the woman's handsome features. The flickering shadows gave it a distinctly macabre twist. 'Maybe I oughta see that it don't happen again.' She took a step forward, her scorching gaze shifting downward to the men's nether regions. The cleaver hovered menacingly.

'We didn't mean nothin',' whined Boggs. 'Just a bit of fun, is all.'

'Don't seem too amusing to me,' scowled Marcia.

'I ain't laughin' neither,' Sankey interposed, eager to add his nickel's worth to the proceedings. 'But maybe we oughta let the marshal handle this, boss,' he added, knowing how the woman was prone to rash outbursts.

'Humph!' grunted Marcia. 'Guess you're right at that, Abel. Can't be taking the law into our own hands, can we? More's the pity.' Then turning to Ellie she said, 'You relieve these birds of their hardware, girl, then we'll all march 'em down to the hoosegow.'

Down at the jailhouse, Marshal Brewer was less than sympathetic after learning that it was Ellie Spavin who had been the intended victim. It was only Marcia Tripp's sassy character that forced the lawman to lock up the two miscreants. Otherwise he would have accepted their plea that the girl had led them on.

Nodding a conspiratorial hint, the café proprietor drew the lawman to one side so that they were out of earshot of the others. Her whispered confidentiality soon persuaded Brewer to accept her interpretation of the seedy events.

'You let these critters off the hook, Milt,' she warned, 'and I'll see to it that your wife is made aware of the frequent visits you make to the Red Garter of a night.'

Hands plumped on ample hips, she held the marshal's wilting gaze. A smirking half-smile challenged him to deny the furtive assignations with May Belle Sumner.

No contest. After that, the guy had little choice but to concede.

The next day Ellie began work in the diner. She quickly picked up the routine of serving the tables. After three days Marcia Tripp was decidedly pleased that she had taken on the ex-whore and given her the chance to redeem her tainted reputation.

On the fourth day chance brought Ellie the break for which she had been seeking.

Two members of the town council had ordered breakfast. Hyram Rattsinger and Clark Jarrett were sipping coffee while awaiting their meal. Both were well dressed in tailormade suits. Diamond pins held their neckties in place.

A vigilant observer might have noted,

however, that this was not a social occasion. The two men were clearly not discussing the weather. They were deep in conversation. Intense gesturing from both parties hinted that serious business was being mooted.

Consequently they failed to heed the waitress standing to one side awaiting the chance to refill their empty coffee cups. A good waitress, Ellie had been told, did not interrupt customers while they were talking. Nor did she listen in to private conversations.

Normally, the rattle of cutlery on plates, shouted orders to the kitchen and general hubbub precluded any such eavesdropping. But the confabulation had reached the point where raised voices accompanied by jabbing fingers indicated that a threat was being issued.

Ellie could not fail to pick up certain words even though she was more concerned about her work than the topic under review by the two men. But the gist of their dispute instantly found her paying more attention. Words such as *loan, debt, owing, charade, disclosure and gambling* impinged themselves on to her brain. But it was when the fatter of the two, the bank manager and treasurer of the council, Hyram Rattsinger, addressed the other man that Ellie became convinced she was on to a strong lead in her quest.

'You told me that the money was for a land deal, Mayor Jarrett,' declared the red-faced banker. 'Now I learn that it was to pay off your gambling debts.' Another pudgy finger jabbed at the sweating mayor of Alamagordo. 'If that money is not repaid in seven days, I will inform the rest of the council and have you arrested for fraud.'

Mayor Jarrett! MA!

Ellie's ice-blue peepers bulged as the two men continued with their quarrel unaware of the flash of lightning that had just occurred.

'You have this all wrong, Hyram,' said the mayor, trying to placate his associate. 'This is a good land deal that has been negotiated. And I can assure you that any gambling losses have been paid off.'

'That's not what I've heard,' rasped the fat man. He was unconvinced by the mayor's wheedling denial. 'And I also know that this is not the first time you have owed money to gamblers.' Another prodding finger emphasized Rattsinger's last comment. 'This is your final warning, sir. Pay up or face the consequences. Disgrace and a possible jail term are not to be taken lightly by any man.'

Ellie had been so intent on listening in to the lively discourse that she inadvertantly nudged the table.

For the first time Jarrett realized that she was there.

'What do you want, girl?' he snapped.

'More coffee, gentlemen?' came the timid reply.

A dismissive wave sent her scurrying away, but quickly turning her head she perceived that no suspicions seemed to be harboured about their discussion having been overheard. Waitresses, like saloon swampers, were barely noticed except when their services were required.

The two men had barely touched their food when the banker leapt to his feet. His face was beetroot red. He slammed a pile of change on the table and stamped out, leaving the mayor to mull over the threat of disclosure should he fail to pay his dues.

Jarrett knew there was no way that he could hope to comply with the bank manager's ultimatum. In truth, he had indeed used the bank's loan as a deposit on a land deal. And he still owed money for gambling debts at the Golden Nugget. Added to that was the fact that Jake Mumby from the Lazy Eight horse ranch also wanted paying for that Arab stallion he had bought.

The mayor was in a bother of indecision as to how he was going to smooth the matter over. There were only so many excuses that folks would accept before they hit back. There must be a way of squaring things and coming out with a profit. Just like he always had in the past.

A half-hour passed with the mayor sipping his now cold coffee and pushing the food around his plate. Ellie kept a close eye on the jasper as she moved between the tables dispensing food and cheery smiles. At last she summoned the nerve to approach the town's leading official once again.

'Food not to your liking, sir?' she asked in a low voice.

The man did not look up, continuing to play with his fork.

'Not that hungry this morning,' he muttered. 'Things on my mind.' *I can understand that*, mused Ellie to herself. 'Town problems that ain't no concern of your'n.' *That's where you're wrong, mister*, the girl felt like saying. But she bit back the retort. Gingerly she placed the bill on the table beside his plate.

The mayor signed it with a morose, 'Put it on my tab.'

Ten minutes went by before Jarrett

hoisted himself out of the chair and moved towards the door.

Before he had chance to leave the diner he felt his arm being held in a firm grip.

'A quiet word if you please, Mr Mayor.' It was the quiet yet insistent voice of Marcia Tripp. 'It is some time since you cleared your slate,' she said. 'It would be much appreciated if you could remedy that situation, as soon as possible.' A resolute eye held the official in a tight, determined grip.

Clark Jarrett had become used to approaches of this sort of late. He had a primed response for such enquiries.

'Have no fear, Miss Tripp,' he breezed. A loose smile was aimed at appeasing the brisk enquiry. 'You will be recompensed within the week.'

The café-owner was not so sure. She cast a puzzled frown at the mayor's back as he departed. There was something not quite right here. Although she could not figure out what was bugging her.

No further time was allowed for the doubts to take root as the hustle and bustle of running a busy enterprise took precedence.

Mayor Jarrett headed straight back to his apartment on Fourth Street. It was occupied rent-free, a perk that he had instigated upon gaining office. At least that was one place for which he didn't owe any money. Things in that department were rapidly getting out of hand.

The bleak situation wasn't helped by the fact that Mace Gifford had not been apprehended following the escape instigated by the bogus hangman. That issue was a constant thorn in his side. As long as the critter was at large, Jarrett could not rest easy.

He threw off his boots and plumped down in an armchair. A handy decanter of best Scotch whisky stood invitingly on the adjacent table. He poured himself a stiff measure downing the contents in a single draught. Peering round the sumptuous living room adorned with the rich trappings redolent of success, he was loath to give it all up without a fight.

Something drastic would have to be done, and quickly. But he was fast running out of options. Debts were piling up faster than drunks on Independence Day. And the rats were nipping at his heels.

Resting his feet on a stool, cigar in one hand, Mayor Jarrett replenished his glass and set to thinking.

'Now then, Clark,' he mumbled to himself imbibing the second glass of whisky at a more sedate pace. 'You came out on top after selling off those fake government bonds in Dallas. Surely this business ain't beyond the figuring of a sharp dude like you.'

Another hour passed before he had come to the conclusion that only one course of action was left open to him. Most of the money he owed was to the saloon owner. That unsavoury fact meant he would have to somehow get hold of the IOU located in the office safe of the Golden Nugget saloon. Cazz Weinberg always kept important documents and his takings up there.

It was now Sunday morning.

More than enough time to retrieve the IOU. Once he had that in his possession, Weinberg could go sing for his money. Without any proof, it would be the dubious word of a saloon owner against that of the well-respected Mayor of Alamagordo. No contest. And there was sure to be enough dough in the safe to satisfy Rattsinger.

The neat thing was, he didn't even have to break in to Weinberg's safe. The careless saloon keeper had left the key on a table in the office during one of their all-night poker sessions. When he had left the room to obtain another bottle of Scotch, Jarret slipped it into his pocket.

Now its acquisition would pay dividends.

Another thought struck the cunning official as he went over the scheme in his mind. It would be necessary to throw the blame for the robbery on to somebody else, just like he had with that greenhorn kid. A leery grimace twisted his hard features. He knew exactly to whom the finger of guilt was going to point.

The bartender of the Golden Nugget was known to enjoy betting on the weekly horse race for which Alamagordo was well known throughout the southwest. Only the previous week Al Bundy had asked Jarrett for a loan of fifty dollars to lay on a certain winner. The mayor had agreed on the understanding that he would receive twenty per cent of the winnings.

The nag had come in fourth.

Just like that fat toady of a bank manager, Jarrett had given his debtor a week to pay. But the mayor knew that he personally had much more to lose. Nevertheless, a few dropped hints here and there would get folks thinking when Bundy's employer was robbed.

Jarrett smiled to himself. He helped himself to another shot of whisky and sat back, going over in his mind the details of his plan of action. Sleep was out of the question. He was too keyed up. Key being the operative word. He smiled at the notion.

This strategy was going to clear things up once and for all.

11

Mixed Fortunes

After leaving the Cabrio Trading Post, El Camaleon headed north-east.

The Sacramento range of mountains lay at the far side of an arid dust plain that saw little rainfall. Catclaw, sage-brush and mesquite grew alongside the dominant creosote bush. This last often reached a height of five feet, its yellow flowers offering a splash of colour that brightened the dullness of the desert terrain.

Clumps of cholla cactus offered a home for wrens. The observant traveller might even catch a glimpse of the comedic road runner.

The variety of flora and fauna held no interest for Manuel Esteban. Revenge and perhaps a quick profit if he struck lucky were of paramount importance to the killer.

Crossing the plain from east to west was the main highway connecting Silver City to Hobbs, on the border with Texas. The outlaw knew from past forays that the weekly stage was due around noon of the following day. Being so close, it would be a pity to pass up the chance of some much needed lucre.

Normally, El Camaleon would have held up the stage accompanied by two or three partners. Being alone would need a much more cautious approach.

It was late afternoon when he reached the wellworn trail.

All around, the terrain was virtually flat. No chance of catching the driver unawares here. To the west the landscape offered no hiding-place to mount a surprise ambush. Only to the east did a possibility present itself. In the distance the elongated upthrust of the Artesia Ridgeback crossed the trail at right angles. The stagecoach could only negotiate the saw-toothed obstruction by passing through a narrow gap known as Chinook Cutting.

This was where he would bait the trap.

A patient *hombre* where the acquisition of money was concerned, the bandit settled down in the lee of the boulder-strewn ridge.

The following morning found him atop a low shelf overlooking the gap. Rifle at the ready, he hunkered down to await the weekly stagecoach. An hour later he glanced at his gold-plated Hunter pocket watch, which showed both hands pointing due north. It was noon. And right on time, he spotted a plume of pale-yellow dust chasing the red Overland towards the cutting.

Esteban levered a round into his rifle and positioned himself ready for his first shot.

Fifteen minutes passed before the sturdy Concord rumbled into the narrow cutting. A driver and shotgun guard were perched up top, bouncing in synchronization with the swaying coach. It was halfway along the quarter-mile ravine when the sound of gunfire bounced off the vertical walls of the cut.

The ambusher smiled as the shotgun rider threw up his arms and tumbled out of his seat, hitting the ground on the far side of the coach.

A second shot followed immediately after. It lifted the driver's hat into the air, where it floated like a kite before settling on the top of an organpipe cactus.

'Haul up on them leathers or the next bullet is a killing shot.'

The cool yet decisive command was lent additional emphasis as the grim words echoed around the cutting. Muttonchop Stoker was given no choice but to obey. His sidekick had bitten the dust, and Muttonchop was in no hurry to join him.

He hauled back on the reins, dragging the coach to a shuddering standstill. 'Now throw down your hardware and grab air.'

The gunman remained on top of the

ridge, only his bare head in view. He had chosen the site of the heist well. There was no room for the lumbering coach to manoeuvre. The only way out of the cutting was forward.

Esteban did not give the coach driver or its occupants any chance to consider retaliating.

'Anybody sticks their head out of the window, it gets blown away. Savvy?' The potent threat was accompanied by another two shots that chipped wood fragments from the side of the cumbersome vehicle. 'You on top. Toss that strongbox down!'

The heavy ironbound chest hit the ground with a dull thud. A ringtailed raccoon darted across in front of the nervous horses, disappearing into a clump of prickly pear.

Esteban's whole attention was focused on the driver. Normally if he had a gang in attendance, the boys would have frisked the passengers for their valuables. Being alone ruled out any such bravado tactics.

'Now whip up them nags and get outa here,' he shouted. 'And you tell them *plebe* in Alamagordo that it was the famous outlaw, El Camaleon that robbed you.' A series of coarse guffaws echoed through the narrow passage as the Concord clattered into motion. 'Ain't no hoosegow in the south-west can hold on to this bad boy for long.'

Two pistol shots encouraged the driver to keep going when he emerged on to the plain beyond the cutting.

The robber stood atop his lofty perch, rifle carried at the port as he watched the stagecoach disappear along the clearly defined trail. Only when it was out of sight did he descend to ground level to examine his haul.

A couple of well-placed slugs blasted the lock. After toeing open the lid he surveyed the contents watched by a curious kangaroo rat poised on a nearby rock. A genuine smile of pleasure streaked the outlaw's leathery features. His greedy fingers delved inside the box rifling through the stack of greenbacks.

'Must be a couple of grand here,' he eagerly enthused. 'Keep me in five star *señoritas* for a spell down in Chihuahua.'

But first there was the business of dealing with that bounty hunting gringo.

Estaban stuffed the dough into his saddle-bags and mounted up. What delayed his boots from rowelling the cayuse into motion was a groan of pain. He paused, listening. It came again, a drawn-out moan of anguish.

The bandit turned towards the source of the disturbing noise. He gave a curse of frustration. So the guard had survived.

'Am I losing my touch? Or does that carbine need resetting?' he growled to himself.

Esteban nudged his mount over to where the dying man was lying on his back. He raised a weak arm, a plea for assistance.

'You want help, gringo?' the bush-whacker asked.

The man's rolling eyes signalled an affirmative.

The bandit thoughtfully considered the man's plight for a few seconds before nodding his agreement.

'You are right, *amigo*. So let no man accuse the great El Camaleon of not showing mercy when it is required. How can any man allow another to suffer in this blistering heat?' Slowly he drew his pistol. The injured man's eyes bulged as two more slugs were pumped into his body. 'Now you are free from all pain, *señor*. And you have El Camaleon to thank. Or you would be able to if you were still alive.'

The bizarre sound of manic laughter rippled around Chinook Cutting as the killer enjoyed his little joke. Then uttering a gleeful howl, he spurred away towards the distant upthrust of the Sacramento Mountains.

* * *

For the rest of her shift Ellie was on tenterhooks. She could not wait to saddle up and let Mace and his brother in on her suspicions. Just as she left the diner around five in the afternoon the weekly stagecoach pounded down the main street.

It was going at a much faster lick than was safe for a busy thoroughfare. Something was clearly amiss. People scattered in all directions. Dogs yelped as clouds of dust rose into the fetid air.

Muttonchop Stoker was leaping off the driver's seat even before the coach had juddered to a standstill. Ignoring the howls of protest and queries regarding his dangerous driving, he hurried into the Overland office to report the robbery and its perpetrator.

Within minutes the dire episode at Chinook Cutting was common knowledge and being passed from mouth to mouth. Gasps of alarm greeted the news that the infamous brigand had escaped the hangman in Las Cruces. Now there were two killers at large.

But why had the bushwhacker made a point of revealing his identity?

Announcing that it was he, El Camaleon, who had robbed the stagecoach was an act of foolhardiness.

Ellie Spavin was the only person in town who had figured out the answer to that poser. This was due to the fact that she had inside information.

The killer must have known that the bounty hunter Montero, who had delivered him up to the law, was himself heading back to Alamagordo. Now the Mexican bandit wanted revenge. Equally important in El Camaleon's warped mind, however, must be the notion that he wanted his quarry to know who was now engaged in the hunting.

With these two vital pieces of information to impart, Ellie was desperate to let her associates in on the score.

Leaving town during daylight hours was fraught with hazards. She could not afford to have any witnesses to her departure. Consequently it was well after midnight when the girl slid out of the back door above the diner and down the steps to her waiting horse.

Gentling the young sorrel, she led it away so as not to awaken her employer. Only when she was well clear of the immediate cluster of buildings did she mount up. The milky white disc of a full moon lit her trail across the uneven landscape.

Much as she would have preferred to urge the horse to a gallop, Ellie forced herself to maintain a slower pace to avoid any unforeseen mishaps. The false dawn was creeping over the eastern horizon when she eventually reached the camp established by the two Gifford brothers.

* * *

Clark Jarrett likewise had waited until the early hours before carrying out his nefarious scheme to erase his debts once and for all.

Sneaking through the darkly silent backlots behind the town's main concourse, he approached the rear of the saloon with some trepidation. Apart from that unfortunate business with Honest Luke Torrance, Mayor Jarrett's illicit activities had been of the 'clean hands' variety: no violent hold-ups, or scurrilous gunlaw. He much preferred to use brain rather than brawn to achieve his dubious ends.

And it had paid dividends, although he was clearly not averse to gunplay if there was no other way out. Break-ins and violence, however, were anathema to a trickster such as Jarrett: a last resort. The current dilemma had left him with no choice. He had to get the IOU and money, and quickly, otherwise his respectable cover would be blown.

Tiptoeing up the back stairs, he entered the upper floor of the Golden Nugget saloon. He paused for a brief second in the corridor and listened. Only the steady drip-drip from a leaking faucet broke into the heavy silence.

The sudden howling of a cat somewhere outside set his strained nerves on edge. Sooner this business was concluded the better. He felt like a square peg in a round hole. Skulking around like a petty thief was not his style.

The door to the office opened to his touch. Jarrett gave a tut of derision accompanied by a scornful shake of the head. Weinburg had not even locked up.

He pushed through into the inner sanctum, quickly closed the window blinds and lit an oil lamp. The safe was over in the far corner. He hooked out the all-important key, and slipped it into the lock. A deep intake of breath, then he slowly turned the key. With a gentle click the tumblers inside dropped and the heavy iron door swung open.

Avaricious eyes devoured the contents. The robber's mouthed dropped open. There was more than $8,000 inside, neatly stacked in bundles. Far more than he had anticipated. The fool had not bothered to bank his takings for at least two weeks.

And there on one side was the IOU,

which he quickly grabbed and stuck in his pocket.

Jarret chuckled aloud. This was much better than he had expected.

He grabbed a hessian sack from a desk drawer and stuffed the notes inside.

That was when a gruff voice struck him with the force of a stampeding buffalo herd.

'What in tarnation is going on here?'

The whiskey-soured vocals of Sleepy Joe Rammidge, the saloon swamper, cut through the tense atmosphere. He was drunk, but not enough to prevent him eyeballing the intruder. 'What the heck are you doing in the boss's private safe, Mayor?' he hollered, still unable to comprehend the obvious significance of his discovery.

Rammidge had been returning from his weekly roll with a Mexican cleaner he had taken up with when he noticed the faint glimmer coming from the boss's office window. The swamper occupied a cot in the back storeroom of the saloon and figured that Weinberg must have inadvertently left the light on.

It came as a jolting shock to his soused brain when he discovered the high-profile thief at work. The swamper fumbled for the gun stuck in his belt. But Sleepy Joe's nickname had been well earned.

In contrast, Jarrett was stone-cold sober. And he had not risen to his current position of pre-eminence in Alamagordo by panicking. A Colt Lightning appeared in his hand. The appearance of the gun galvanized the inebriated swamper into action. An instinct for survival drove him to launch his stick-thin frame at the robber.

Without hesitation Jarrett pumped three bullets into the struggling swamper. The noise was deafening in the confined space. Smoke filled the room. And through the haze, Rammidge's bullet-riddled torso tumbled into the kneeling figure of the mayor.

Jarrett cursed as he tried to extricate

himself from beneath the bloody corpse.

Now the fat was well and truly in the fire. This was the last thing he had anticipated. Too late for regrets. Finding himself coated with the sticky red life force of his victim, he knew that getting away unseen was now an urgent priority.

Already the crash of gunfire had alerted a wandering pack of hounds. Their raucous barking was sure to have awoken the marshal, whose office was right across the street.

Grasping hold of the money sack, Jarrett left the building by the way he had entered. It took him ten minutes to reach his home.

The gunfire had indeed awoken more than just the town marshal. Lights were coming on all over the place. Jarrett had been forced to take shelter as citizens peered out of windows. Some even ventured out of their homes. Gunfire would normally not have attracted such attention. But at this hour of the morning it was distinctly unusual and called for investigation.

Dark shadows and recesses helped the frightened killer to evade detection. It was with a great sense of relief that he stumbled through the back door of his house. Sucking in great gulps of air, his pounding chest heaving, Clark Jarrett at last felt safe.

His trembling frame slid to the floor. He remained there until his heart rate had simmered down to something like normal. With a shaking hand he sought to unfasten his necktie. It felt like it was about to throttle him. That was when he made a dreadful discovery.

Where was his diamond stickpin?

Panicking, his hands desperately riffled throgh his clothes. Nothing.

Bubbles of moisture popped on his forehead as the awful truth punched him in the guts. Jarrett took off his spectacles and mopped away the sweat. During his struggle with the dying body of Joe Rammidge, the stickpin must have been torn off.

So now it was lying on the floor at the scene of the crime.

Only two men in Alamagordo were known to sport such an ostentatious display of bad taste. Hyram Rattsinger was unlikely to have lost his. And mutterings in respect of Jarrett's debts were already being voiced in various quarters. Marshal Brewer couldn't help but find the twinkling bauble. Its discovery was, therefore, bound to point the unerring finger of suspicion at the town mayor.

In that event, there was only one course of action open to him: immediate flight before a delegation burst through the door and frogmarched him down to the jailhouse. Already Clark Jarrett could feel the hangman's noose tightening around his neck. And in his case there would be no guardian angel waiting to save him from the Grim Reaper's welcoming handshake.

The need for urgent action in this dire situation focused the mayor's thoughts.

After a quick change of clothes and a hasty packing of gear he went outside to the back stable to saddle the Arab stallion. Within fifteen minutes he was ready to leave. His hand brushed the hessian sack fastened to the pommel.

At least he now had a substantial grubstake to start up afresh in another town, maybe even another territory.

Jarrett tweaked the ears of the magnificent piece of horseflesh as he mounted up.

'Pity we won't be taking part in next week's race, Lightning,' he whispered in the stallion's ear. 'You would have been a surefire victor and the winnings would have paid everyone off.' Jarrett shrugged regretfully. 'Too darned late now, due to that interfering hog, Sleepy Rammidge.'

Giving a final wistful glance at his opulent residence the fugitive nudged Lightning forward into the dim mist of early morning.

12

Stakeout

After she had arrived at the secluded camp set up by the Giffords, Ellie quickly related what she had overheard and voiced her suspicions. On hearing that the man in question was none other than Clark Jarrett and that he was the mayor of Alamagordo, Mace slammed a bunched fist into the palm of his hand.

That jasper was having a shindig in the saloon the night I was there,' declared the younger Gifford with vigour. 'At the time I didn't know he was the mayor. Some dude just said he was from the town council. Turned out it was his birthday. They were causing a right old hoohah.' His brow furrowed on recalling the incident. 'Torrance the gambler kept glowering across at the guy. I figured that the ruckus they were making was distracting his concentration.'

Clem nodded his agreement. 'Now we know it was on account of the dough he was owed,' he concluded.

'Sure was,' concurred Mace. 'After I was thrown out of the saloon, Torrance must have pulled the rat aside and threatened to make his debts public knowledge if'n he didn't pay up.'

Ellie stroked her paramour's hair to sooth his rising anger.

'And I know that Miss Tripp at the diner was concerned over the mayor's unpaid bills,' she added.

'There were probably a heap of other creditors on his back at the same time,' said Clem. 'And most likely still are. Some other poor sap might well be in his gunsight right now.'

'Then we ain't got time to lose,' hollered Mace, rising to his feet.

'Hold on there,' cautioned Clem, laying a restraining hand on his brother's shoulder. 'No sense in going off half-cocked. This needs careful thought and a foolproof plan of action. Otherwise it could all blow up in our faces.'

'I agree with Clem,' Ellie urged her quick-tempered love. 'Jarrett is a slippery customer and he's got a ruthless streak. One man has been killed already to hide his guilty secret. He'll need careful handling if'n a confession is going to be wormed out of him.'

Sipping black coffee, the three confederates pondered over the problem. Time passed quickly. Before they knew it, the dawn chorus was breaking in upon their tense deliberations. Numerous early risers hooting and cawing in the dim shadows beyond the dying campfire greeted the new day.

And the trio had still had not come up with a plan.

Then Clem slapped his thighs. He had reached a decision. He rose to his feet and announced bluntly that he was going back to Alamagordo to confront the skunk face to face.

'Set off now and I'll catch him before he wakes up. Force his hand at gunpoint.' He waved away the impassioned protestations of his companions. 'Makes sense. This is my business. I know how to deal with skunks like Mayor Jarrett.' He turned to Mace. 'You and Ellie head for Tomahawk Gap and wait for me there.'

Once they recognized that his mind was set, Ellie gave directions of how to reach the mayor's house. They parted with a promise that he would not return without a full written confession duly signed. The means by which it would be obtained were not discussed.

'You take care,' urged a newly invigorated Mace Gifford, gripping his brother's hand. All the past animosity between the two had been forgotten, buried in a deep hole. 'Ain't no way I want you earning a one-way ticket to Boot Hill on my account.'

Clem returned the fraternal grip. An encouraging smile passed between them. No further words were needed. Clem turned his mount and trotted back down the draw.

He was about halfway to Alamagordo when a rising plume of dust coming towards him caught his attention. Not wishing to encounter any other travellers, he pulled into a small clump of cottonwoods and waited for the rider to pass by. As the other man drew nearer, Clem was able to pick out the the guy's features lit up by the easterly sun.

It came as a distinct shock to see that it was none other than his quarry. Even though he had barely eyeballed the critter for more than a brief spell at the time of the escape, there was no mistaking that waxed moustache.

Gone was the natty suit, the snow-white frilled shirt and red necktie, all topped off by a stiff grey derby. In their place the varmint had opted for the anonymity of dull range gear.

As a bonus. Jarrett had been the only one present at the execution wearing spectacles. The rubies embedded in the gold frame were now winking at him like two extra eyes.

This was a lucky break that required a rapid response.

As he drew closer it became clear that Mayor Jarrett was not merely out for an early morning ride before breakfast. The bedroll and bulging saddlebags pointed to a protracted journey. And what was in that sack tied to the pommel? Could the guy have already been sussed and was now making a break for it while he still had the chance?

There was only one way to find out.

Clem unfastened his lariat and readied the loop. He allowed the unsuspecting rider to pass before emerging from cover. A couple of twirls around his head and the rope was launched. It was a perfect aim, encircling the target's body before he knew what was happening. A sharp tug and the mayor was jerked out of his saddle.

He landed on the ground with a jarring thud. Pinioned by the rope he lay where he had fallen, stunned by the sudden twist in his fortunes. One minute he was jogging along idly contemplating a fresh start, next thing he was grovelling in the dust.

What in thunder had happened?

His question was soon answered as a blunt command cut through the stupor of his addled brain.

'On your feet, *Mister Mayor*!' Clem's tones carried an overlay of mocking derision. 'You have some questions to answer. And if'n I don't receive the right answers, things are gonna get mighty tough for you.'

Before Jarrett had time to recover Clem had removed Jarrett's pistol and stuck it into his own belt. A brutal wrench of the tight rope then encouraged the captive to stumble to his feet.

The spectacles lay on the ground at his feet, still in one piece.

Jarrett blinked. 'At least allow me to wear those,' he spluttered, coughing up a mouthful of grit. 'Can't think straight without them.'

Clem huffed but permitted the stunned man to loosen the rope and bend down to retrieve them.

After setting the eyeglasses on his nose, the mayor peered at his captor. His nose crinkled in puzzlement. Who was this bushwhacker? A common bandit, or . . . ? His gaze flicked nervously towards the sack of money tied to his saddle.

He was given no further time to speculate.

'Recognize me, do you?' Clem snapped, pushing his face forward. Encouragement for Jarrett to respond was supported by a cocked pistol.

The mayor arrowed a look at the speaker. 'Can't say that I do.'

'Then look closer, cos you and I met up in Alamogordo at a certain hanging that didn't quite go according to plan if'n you recall.' A leery grin accompanied this pertinent aid to the mayor's enlightenment.

The penny dropped.

'You!'

'Yep, me!' Clem couldn't restrain a

caustic guffaw at the jasper's shocked expression. 'It was my brother who had been framed for the murder of that gambler. And all the time it was you who carried out the foul deed, on account of debts you couldn't pay.'

Once he was launched on his blistering denouncement of the official's skulduggery, Clem's biting diatribe knew no bounds. He grabbed the quaking rat by the throat and shook him like a dog with a bone. Then, having thrown him to the ground, Clem jammed his revolver up the guy's twitching snout.

'My figuring is that he had threatened to expose you. Mace just happened to turn up at the right time. Issuing a threat of his own when the gambler tried to cheat him was a lucky break you just couldn't resist.' A brusque cuff round the ear urged a confession from the guilty felon. 'Ain't that the durned truth, you miserable bastard? And now it appears you are up to the same tricks again. Owing money to all and sundry in Alamagordo.'

But Clark Jarrett was no milksop. He quickly shook off the effects of this sudden turnaround in his circumstances. Recovering his dented composure, the devious critter pressed home a spirited denial of the accusation. Admitting to his crime would surely end with his own neck in the noose. But how did this jigger know about the build-up of his other debts?

Brazenly, he attempted to bluff his way out of the accusation.

'I have no idea what you are talking about,' he countered bluntly. 'You are the one who has broken the law, by helping a convicted murderer to escape justice. And now you are accosting an elected official going about his lawful business.'

Clem gritted his teeth. He should have known that the skunk would deny all knowledge of his felonious activities. Then his gaze settled once again on the heavy sack.

'Then let's have a look-see at what you're toting.'

'Touch any of my possessions and I will see to it that you are hunted down and a hefty price put on your head,' blustered Jarrett, trying desperately to assert some authority of his own into the proceedings.

Clem — Montero the infamous bounty hunter — couldn't help but laugh out loud at such a threat.

The levity was short-lived as he thrust the blackguard aside. He reached for the sack, stuck his hand inside and removed a wad of greenbacks.

'Now what have we here?' he smirked, waving the money in the mayor's face. 'You call this going about your lawful business?' Not waiting for a reply, he pressed on. 'My bet is that this is stolen money and you're trying to make a run for it before all the creditors gather.'

Realizing that the game was up, Jarrett tried to make a deal with the bounty hunter.

'There's ten grand in there,' he said. 'How about we split it down the middle? I ride off and we're both winners. What d'you say?'

His eyes fluttered hopefully.

'Only one problem with that, Mayor,' Clem said, stroking his chin as if in two minds whether to accept the offer. He gave the official a mirthless grin. 'I could take all of this and leave you here. After all, it's me that's holding the gun.' The smile dissolved, replaced by an icy gleam. 'And there's still the matter of your signing a confession to clear my brother. And when you've done that, we're both going back to town so that everybody can see what a lowdown rat you really are.'

'Never,' answered the mayor vehemently. 'Sign that and I'm a dead man.'

Clem slung a stiff punch that connected with the guy's jaw. Blood gushed from a burst lip as he went down.

'You're a dead man if'n you don't,' snarled the incensed bounty hunter.

'And my way will be infinitely less pleasant.'

'Go to hell!' came back the blunt retort.

'Believe me when I tell you, mister, that's where you're a-going.' Clem brought the gun barrel down sharply on Jarrett's head. 'When I've finished, you'll be praying to sign that confession.' But the critter didn't hear the final threat. He was lying prone on the ground, unconscious.

Within fifteen minutes, Clem had his victim staked out. Spread-eagled face up. Another ten minutes passed before he had found what he was seeking among a cluster of rocks. Careful extraction of the reptile was needed to avoid being caught by its venomous fangs.

The lively rattlesnake was also staked out so that its angry lunge would miss the pinioned man's head by a mere whisker. Each time the rattler struck, the victim would have to move his head slightly to one side. An ever more tiring necessity as time passed.

Chopping off the snake's tail bones meant that the deadly creature would slowly bleed to death, becoming weaker but more irate. Victims could sometimes survive for days. There was no telling which might succeed first — snake or man.

Appropriately called the sidewinder's kiss, it was a favourite punishment of the Mescaleros. Clem had seen the grim torment administered to an old partner who had been captured while having his way with a young squaw.

It was unfortunate that Buckie Leeson had chosen the chief's daughter with whom to indulge his passion. Mimbreno had not been well pleased. He wanted full retribution for such a desecration of his only child. Clem could only watch helplessly from a secret vantage point overlooking the place of execution. A vain hope remained that a chance to save his partner would present itself.

None did. Buckie lasted twelve hours

before the dying snake had the final say in the matter.

Both man and beast were left where they lay, their bones picked clean by the desert scavengers. Clem always made a point of calling at the gruesome site when passing that way. It was a poignant reminder never to take the Indian tribes for granted, or anyone else, for that matter.

Clem had no intention of leaving Jarrett to that fate. He was sure that after a few hours to sweat it out the duplicitous villain would be willing to sign anything.

He mounted up and spurred off, intending to catch up with his partners before they had ridden too far.

13

A Break for Jarrett

The sun was well on his journey across the blue sky when Manuel Esteban drew his mount to a halt. A sound alien to the bleak landscape had assailed his ears. Straining, he waited for it to recur. A minute passed, then another. He was just about to shrug it off as a figment of his imagination when a bloodcurdling holler ripped the silence apart.

It was coming from the far side of some rocks.

The outlaw screwed up his nose, reasoning that out here in the wilderness, it had to come from an animal in pain. On further reflection, however, he judged that this was much more akin to a human cry for help.

Gingerly the Mexican nudged his horse forward. Revolver cocked and ready, he carefully skirted the rocks.

The sight that met his narrowed gaze was awesome to behold.

A gringo staked out with a rattlesnake doing its level best to reach him, so far without success, although that outcome could only be a matter of time. Esteban had heard about the 'sidewinder's kiss'. But this, was the first time he had witnessed it in practice. Certainly, it was not a sight to inspire calming thoughts and settle twanging nerves.

Restless eyes panned the surrounding terrain. Were them damned Apaches still in the vicinity? His fingers edgily tapped the butt of his pistol. There were no signs that Indians had been here. Indeed, all the indications pointed to shod hoofs, which suggested that his own kind were responsible.

Esteban moved closer. His shadow hovered over the tethered captive.

The man looked up, a bloodshot eye fastening on to the rider.

The moan turned into an impassioned plea when the victim realized that he was no longer alone.

'Help me!' came the croak appeal. 'For pity's sake, don't leave me here.'

Esteban cast a quick glance at the staked-out man, then flicked his gaze to the swaying twist of the ugly head little more than a foot away. Suddenly the snake lunged yet again, its dripping fangs reaching for the enemy forcing the man to jerk his head away.

Another howl of anguish burst from the gringo's dry throat. The tormented wail sounded more like a vixen in heat. The captive's pinioned body arched in panic.

Now that the threat of an Indian attack seemed unlikely Esteban relaxed. Resting his hands on the saddle horn, he leaned over to get a better look at the gladiatorial combat from a safe distance. A grim smirk creased the Mexican's swarthy features.

'And why should I do that, *señor*?' he asked lightly. 'Maybe you a bad fella who deserves to suffer. But El Camaleon is a merciful *hombre*. Perhaps I could make things easier for you with this.' He waved the pistol menacingly. 'A bullet between the eyes would certainly ease your misery.'

Jarrett's eyes widened. So this was the much-feared bandit. Any hope of being rescued rapidly faded.

'No, please.' mouthed the captive, desperately shaking his head, an action that only served to irritate the snake even further. Another attack followed, only just missing the victim's bobbing head by a paper's width.

Esteban couldn't resist a chuckle. 'Somebody sure has it in for you, *señor*. Now I wonder to myself why that should be.'

'Set me free and I can make you rich,' burbled a terrified Clark Jarrett: a desperate man clutching at straws. 'Ain't that a good enough reason?' The hope of freedom forced the words out in a staccato babble.

'The ramblings of a dead man,' scoffed the outlaw.

'It's true!' hollered Jarrett, desperation lending impetus to the impassioned supplication. 'What have you to lose?'

Esteban's brow creased in thought. Maybe this gringo was telling the truth. He decided to play along and slipped the gun back into its holster.

'So that is why you have ended up like this,' was the cautious reply as he dismounted. 'Perhaps I will help you. But how do I know that such an offer is not just an idle plea for mercy with no meat?'

'How does ten grand sound?' the tethered man rushed the question out, anxious to maintain the outlaw's interest. 'It was stolen from me. You release me and we can go after the thief together and split the loot.'

Esteban coolly digested the proposal. Sweat coated the captive's face as he silently urged the hovering villain to set him free.

But the Mexican was in no rush. He was thoroughly enjoying the gringo's torment. If what he had claimed was true, such an amount was most certainly worth pursuing. He could go after the bounty hunter Montero later. And if this dude was lying, a bullet in the guts would be his reward.

Eventually, after what seemed like half a dozen lifetimes to Jarrett, the Mexican nodded. He drew his gun and drilled a couple of slugs into the hovering snake, which thrashed against its bonds before falling still. Then he drew his knife and cut through the four ropes binding the captive.

Jarrett immediately scuttled away from the loathsome reptile before rubbing some life back into his aching limbs.

'Water, water,' he wheezed, reaching out a hand. The tongue filling his mouth felt like a lump of dried-up leather.

His rescuer tossed over a half-filled bottle, the contents of which the released man drank down in a single draught. Looking up Jarrett stared at the menacing barrel of a six-shooter.

'About that money, *señor*,' hissed Esteban. 'I hope for your sake this is no trick. I would hate to return you to your recent fix.'

'Trust me when I tell you that the dough is real enough,' Jarrett assured his saviour. 'All we have to do is pick up the rat's trail and follow it.'

'That might not be so easy,' replied Esteban, his trained eye following the line of departing hoof prints. He pointed a finger towards the east. 'He is headed for the mountains. And seeing as you have no horse, we will have to ride double. That will slow us up.'

Without waiting for any response, Esteban continued. 'So who is this mysterious bandit who has robbed you?'

'I don't know his name,' said Jarrett. He dusted himself down and retrieved his battered hat. 'Only that he was the critter that helped free a prisoner in Alamagordo who was due to be hanged.'

The mayor purposely omitted his part in the seedy affair including how he had come by the money.

'I figured they'd be out of the territory by now.' Jarrett hurried on trying to justify how he had come to be in possession of such a large sum. 'I've just sold my share of a saloon in town and was heading for Roswell to start up afresh.'

But Esteban was not listening. Neither was he concerned who this fellow was or how he had acquired the money.

His face was set like stone. This robber had to be Montero. And now the guy was ten grand up. Surely he would now return to his hideout in the Sacramentos until the hue and cry died down.

It seemed that Lady Luck was sitting on his shoulder. Now he knew for sure where the bounty hunter was heading. And by getting rid of the critter, he — Manuel Esteban, the infamous bandit known as El Camaleon — would be handsomely rewarded for his efforts.

'And what is your name, *amigo*?' asked the bandit, intimating that they were now on equal terms. In truth, the outlaw had no intention of sharing the loot once acquired. This fellow would meet the same fate as Montero. But until that time arrived, he would require the gringo's help to achieve his ends.

'They call me . . . ' Jarrett concealed the momentary pause with a cough. He had no wish to divulge his real name in case this guy had heard of him. Better to remain incognito. 'Erm, Buckskin Frank is my handle.'

'*Buenos dias*, Buckskin,' warbled the outlaw, arrowing his new partner with a sceptical eye. He knew perfectly well that the guy was lying. But no matter. He would be a useful extra gun when he flushed out his quarry.

'And I am Manuel Esteban of Chihuahua.' He held out a hand. The fixed smile on his face was coldly menacing. 'Perhaps we should rest up awhile before setting out in pursuit of your bushwhacker?'

Jarrett nodded his agreement.

Soon a fire was burning. A greasy

mess of refried beans and fatback sizzled in a black frying-pan. On being presented with a plate of the obnoxious repast, Jarrett felt it prudent to remain tight-lipped. He shovelled down the food, hiding the vile taste with numerous mugs of coffee which was thankfully hot and strong.

A half-hour later, the unlikely pair set off heading east. At first they followed the single trail of hoof-prints, but they were soon forced to pursue their own course when the sign veered away and vanished across a rocky plateau. No amount of searching and back-tracking brought it to light again.

The setback did not bother Esteban unduly as he knew exactly where the robber was heading.

Perched on the bedroll tied behind the saddle, Jarrett clung on to the Mexican's broad back as they jolted along. It was a decidedly uncomfortable position that soon became almost unbearable. Only the thought of recovering his lost grubstake and escaping the hangman's noose kept him going.

When they stopped beside a chattering creek to refill the canteen, Jarrett slid to the ground. Stiff and sore, he could barely move.

'Something bothering you, *hombre*?' Esteban smirked and lit up a cigar.

'Any chance of me riding up front?' replied Jarrett meekly.

But Esteban was unsympathetic to his new partner's woe. The Mexican's response was an uproarious laugh.

'Your back end is hurting, eh?' he said, knowing full well the mayor's predicament. Jarrett nodded hopefully. 'Well,' replied his partner musing on this information. 'You always have the choice of walking, Buckskin.' He spoke with mock seriousness. 'We have not far to go from here. Maybe another two days' travel is all.'

Clark Jarrett, alias Buckskin Frank, groaned aloud.

At that moment, Estaban leapt to his feet.

'But luck may be on your side today,

my good friend.'

He was staring upstream. A lone sourdough prospector was leading a burro along the opposite bank of the creek. His eyes were completely focused on the sandy edges of the watercourse. Clearly the old jasper was searching for signs of paydirt and had not seen the two travellers.

'When he comes level, you call him over,' said Esteban. 'I will do the rest.'

The outlaw slid out of sight behind a clump of juniper trees.

Five minutes later the prospector was on the opposite bank and had still not cottoned to the fact that he was not alone.

'Fancy joining me,' Jarrett called across to the searching miner. The little guy almost jumped out of his skin. 'I'm just about to heat up a fresh pot of coffee.'

'Where in thunder did you come from?' enquired the startled jasper.

'You were too engrossed in eyeballing the creek to notice,' replied Jarrett making to unfasten the store sack tied to Esteban's horse. 'What d'yuh say? I could do with a spot of company for a spell.'

'Much obliged, stranger.' The miner smiled and splashed across the shallow waters. He held out a grubby paw. 'The name's Panhandle Charlie Grubb. 'Ain't seen a living soul in six weeks and that's a durned fact. I'd almost forgotten what a human voice sounded like.'

And you ain't gonna hear no more, Estaban muttered to himself as he emerged from cover behind the old-timer.

Being a lone prospector, the guy would not be missed. The cold-blooded killer gripped the lethal bowie knife by its bone handle and crept up behind the unsuspecting guy, quiet as a desert fox. The razor-edged blade glinted in the overhead sunlight.

Panhandle Charlie didn't stand a chance.

A single driving jab and the ten-inch blade ground through the guy's ribs and up into his heart. With no more than a brief exhalation of punctured air the old-timer breathed his last, sliding to the ground in a heap of dirty rags. Placing a boot on the dead body, the Mexican dragged out the blade with a sickening squelch and wiped it on the guy's trousers.

Not a trace of remorse or pity was displayed.

'There's your transport, Buckskin.' He pointed at the grazing burro. Then he proceeded to search the dead man for any valuables. The only thing of note was a small leather pouch containing half a dozen nuggets of gold. 'This can be my reward for saving your mangy hide,' he said to his partner, and pocketed the loot.

Once Jarrett had waded across the creek and led the pack animal back, they both examined the prospector's worldly goods for anything worth keeping. The haul was meagre. Not much to show for a lifetime of mooching about in the wilderness.

Soon after, the pair of ne'er-do-wells broke camp and were on the move once again.

* * *

Clem Gifford caught up with his brother and Ellie Spavin a little before noon. After he had told them of the bizarre change in circumstances, the obvious course now was to swing their horses around and retrace their steps. Clem was confident that a signed confession could easily be extracted in return for releasing the killer from his torment.

As chance would have it, the two factions passed each other no more than a mile apart. Yet neither was aware of the other's presence.

However, because of Jarrett's unorthodox form of transport, the pair of desperadoes were moving at a much slower pace. This did not worry Esteban unduly as he was confident of his quarry being ensconced at the supposedly secret hideout when they reached Tomahawk Canyon the following day.

Meanwhile, the other three had reached the place where Clem had claimed to have staked out the killer mayor of Alamagordo.

The sun had now dipped behind the San Andres range to the west. Darkening bubbles of cloud dusted the jagged peaks of the mountains. Shadows were slowly edging their cautious way across a flat sandy patch. It would soon be nightfall. Yet there was still enough light to observe that the site of the supposed stakeout was empty.

Finding only the shattered body of a dead snake and four pieces of severed rope was a stunning blow. Clem shook his head in bewilderment. This changed everything.

'There is no way that Jarrett could have escaped alone,' he stressed fervently, then he pointed at the snake. 'And look at that rattler. It's been blasted by a shooter.'

'Somebody must have lit upon him,' Mace averred, peering around warily. He half-expected the mysterious benefactor to start blasting at them. 'That means there's at least two varmints out there some place.'

'It also means that your signed confession has flown out of the window,' added Ellie, further contributing to the downcast mood that had settled over the trio. 'Jarrett and his goddamned saviour could be any place by now.'

The uncharacteristic expletive was received with morose nods from Clem and his brother.

'Only thing we can do now is head direct for the hideout and keep our heads down for a spell,' Clem expressed firmly. He tapped the hessian sack. 'At least we have this dough to get us started some place else when the fuss has died down.'

'It still leaves me with a false charge of murder hanging over my head,' mumbled a glum Mace Gifford. 'And like as not there'll be a Wanted dodger out for my capture — dead or alive!'

'Not while I'm still breathing free, little brother,' asserted Clem vehemently.

'And don't forget me,' Ellie interjected, consoling the distraught kid with a tender stroke of his arm. 'Ain't no way that I'll abandon you now. We're a team now, right?'

'Sure thing, Ellie.'

Mace forced a tight smile. But his mood remained downcast.

Clem knew that time was not on their side. Those guys could be anywhere. The sooner they were safe in Tomahawk Canyon the better he would feel.

'Let's ride, folks,' he urged. 'No sense hanging around here.'

14

Tomahawk Canyon

'How long do you figure we need to stay cooped up in this old shack?'

Mace Gifford's nose wrinkled at the musty odour that greeted the trio as they pushed open the cabin door. A rat scuttled out between his legs and disappeared into a clump of stinkweed.

'Don't knock it,' Clem admonished his brother, although he had to admit the place could certainly benefit from a clean-up. 'There's everything we need here until such time as the hullabaloo dies down.'

'So how long is that gonna be?' pressed Mace.

'A couple of weeks, then we can head east into Texas.'

Meanwhile Ellie had found a couple of brooms in a closet. 'Instead of turning up your nose at such high-class accommodation, perhaps you can help get it sorted out.' She thrust the broom into Mace's hand, challenging him to refuse if he dared.

'Glad to know someone has got your measure at last,' chuckled Clem. He delved into the cupboards in search of further supplies.

Some of the sacks of flour had been attacked by rodents and had to be discarded. But most of the goods were still usable. He held up a large tin of peaches in one hand and a bottle of blue-label whiskey in the other.

'I can even supply my guests with luxuries during their stay.'

Mace had to smile. 'You seem to have things all worked out, don't you?'

'A necessity in my profession.' A serious note terminated the light-hearted banter. 'There have been times when delivering wanted felons to the law brought a hornet's nest down around my ears.'

'How do you mean?' asked Mace.

His brother poured them both a liberal measure of whiskey before elucidating. 'Remember the Jarvis Gang?' Mace nodded. 'After bringing in Monk Jarvis, the leader, the rest of his boys were out to get me. They even posted their own bounty. This place proved its worth until such time as the varmints were themselves hunted down. Since then I've always kept it well stocked with essentials that don't go bad.'

'How did you find the canyon?'

Mace accepted a cigar to complement the drink. They both lit up. Clem drew hard on the thin tube, then exhaled a thin stream of blue smoke before continuing.

'I knew that avoiding the main trails and heading into the mountains was my only hope of evading those boys. Hank Jarvis had sworn to gun me down for dry-gulching his brother. And he had another half-dozen mean-eyed critters to back him up. It was only by chance that I turned down that draw leading to the entrance to the canyon. It was choked with brambles and thornbush.'

Mace was transfixed by his brother's story. Even Ellie had paused in her efforts to make the cabin habitable once again. She sat down next to her lover and grasped his hand.

'Once I had found this hidden bolthole, I returned to the start of the draw and backed up some way to rub out my tracks. The gang couldn't have been more than three hours behind me. Then I waited.' Clem sucked in a deep mouthful of air. 'That three hours felt like a month. It was only after sundown that I could relax, knowing that I'd lost them.'

'And that was when you knew you'd found the perfect hideout,' said Ellie.

'So far,' replied Clem. 'Let's hope it stays that way.'

Over the next couple of days the three partners settled into their new accommodation. Ellie was given the only separate room while the brothers bunked down together in the main room. The girl proved to be an admirable cook, doing her best to vary her use of the limited ingredients available.

On the third day disaster struck.

* * *

El Camaleon knew the general location of Tomahawk Canyon. But it took them a full day of searching the numerous dead-end draws and gulches that criss-crossed the rugged fastness of the Sacramentos for him and his unlikely ally to uncover the hidden entrance. And only then through pure luck.

Perhaps it was over-confidence on Clem Gifford's part, having used the secret hideaway so successfuly on previous occasions. Or it might have been carelessness on the part of his companions who failed to take sufficient precautions at the final hurdle. Whatever the reasons, a few hoofprints close to the narrow ravine marking the entrance to Tomahawk Canyon had not been erased.

The Mexican bandit could barely

contain his elation as he jabbed a finger at the vital sign. He punched the air with delight. But he knew that extreme prudence was required from there on.

'No talking, Buckskin,' he whispered, leading the way into the constricted passage. 'unless it's urgent, and only then in a whisper. Savvy?'

Jarrett responded with a curt nod of the head.

He was as pleased to reach their destination as was his partner, in order to regain the stolen grubstake. Although at that moment the need to jettison his punishing means of transport was uppermost in his thoughts. The last three days had been uncomfortable to say the least. His hindquarters had been rubbed raw by the constant twitching of the ungainly brute.

After twenty minutes of cautious progress along the tortuous rift, the duo emerged into a wooded grove. Stands of cottonwood and Douglas fir concealed them from any prying eyes. They pushed through the trees, following the clear set of prints that confirmed the fact that riders had passed this way in the recent past.

Esteban gestured for them to dismount. Leading their horses, the two men tentatively pressed on through the tree cover until they reached the far edge.

Over on the opposite side of the clearing was a cabin. Better still, there was smoke rising from the chimney, indicating a human presence. But of the supposed humans, there was no sign.

Scanning the terrain with a practised eye, Esteban concluded that Montero must be inside the cabin. So how was he going to flush the varmint out?

A frontal assault was out of the question. The open ground between the trees and the cabin provided no cover should they be spotted. However, the occupant might well consider himself to be immune from discovery. Maybe he was even now sleeping off a celebration of having so easily come by a hefty wad of dough.

He kept watch for a further ten minutes. As time passed, the outlaw became convinced that a surprise attack by the two of them across the open sward posed no problems. He was about to voice his plan when the door of the cabin opened and a man stepped out. He wandered over to a well and filled a bucket before returning to the cabin.

It was not Montero. So who was this mysterious gringo?

Buckskin Frank provided the answer.

'That's the jigger that was going to be hanged in Alamagordo and escaped with the connivance of the fella that robbed me,' he trilled. Shock was starkly etched across the mayor's gaping features. 'The two of them must have stuck together.'

Esteban cursed under his breath. This made their task that much harder. Certainly they would have to abandon any idea of a direct attack now.

A more circumspect assessment of the immediate environment followed.

The cabin was situated below a cliff face that stretched for a hundred yards either side. The trees had been cleared to enable miners who once operated here to drive levels inside the rock. It must have been abandoned some considerable time in the past, judging by the rusting paraphernalia scattered about the clearing.

But on the mesa above the cabin, the outlaw noticed a loose cluster of boulders. From this angle, they appeared to be precariously balanced. Just a few well placed rocks rolling down the gradient would dislodge the whole caboodle and an avalanche could be set in motion. They were not quite in line with the cabin below. But all that was needed were a few rocks landing on the roof to drive the occupants outside.

Then some well-placed shots would leave the way open for Esteban to cut them down and grab the dough.

'I have a plan to get them outside,' he announced breezily, 'and it involves you circling round behind the cabin and climbing up on to that mesa.' He arrowed a caustic glower at his partner that brooked no argument. Without waiting for a response, he outlined what Jarrett had to do. 'Once the rocks are on the move, come down and back me up from the side. That should give us a winning hand.'

Jarrett hesitated. He was decidedly nervous of heights.

'You make objection to my plan, *amigo?*' The Mexican's intimidating glare was supported by the Winchester. But knowing that he needed the other man's cooperation, he allowed a benign smile to draw his lips apart. 'You are key to getting the money back and this, I regret, is the only way.'

'I guess so,' mumbled the reluctant rock shifter.

'Then go to it and let us kick some ass,' urged Esteban. 'We have no time to waste,' he added. 'They could decide to leave any time.' A poke of the rifle encouraged Jarrett to shift his butt. '*Salir de prisa*! Hurry up!'

15

Rock 'n' Roll

Almost an hour passed before the burly figure of Clark Jarrett, alias Buckskin Frank, appeared above the loose stack of boulders. During the intervening spell, a girl had emerged from the cabin to feed the horses and empty some rubbish into a ditch. His hated enemy, the bounty hunter Montero, also came outside once to tend to his horse.

Esteban was sorely tempted to put a bullet in the skunk's hide. The only thing that stayed his itchy trigger finger was the fact that the others were still inside the cabin. That meant there were at least three adversaries to deal with. Two more than he had anticipated.

If Frank could get those rocks a-tumbling down that slope, it would give him the element of surprise.

Esteban screwed up his eyes trying to focus in on what his unwanted partner was doing. Silently he prayed that the *mentecato* gringo would not foul things up. A few rocks had been pushed down the slope but none had thus far precipitated an avalanche.

Jarrett then moved further over towards the mid point above the main cluster of rocks. Again he heaved and wrenched. A couple began rolling down the slope. Gathering momentum, they soon crashed into the main body of rocks. More were dislodged to join the tumbling cascade. Clouds of dust rose into the air as the shifting phalanx of boulders rolled towards the lip of the mesa.

Witnessing the surge of movement, Esteban experienced a ripple of euphoria streaming through his veins. The moment of truth was at hand.

Having succeeded in bringing about the avalanche, Jarrett could see that the displacement of the rocks had revealed a narrow fissure slanting down to the flat ground below. Quickly he moved across to the head of the rift. It would entail a steep and rough descent, but was much faster than the route by which he had climbed up.

* * *

Mace was the first to pay heed to the growing rumble.

'What's that noise?' he asked, a forkful of tinned peach hovering next to his open mouth.

Clem stopped cleaning his rifle and listened. For a couple of seconds both their faces registered puzzlement. Then Clem cast his gaze towards the cabin's tar-felted plank roof. A loud thump suddenly resounded through the room. The roof shook but held firm.

'Avalanche!'

The single word galvanized the two men into action as another rock hit the roof. The planks cracked and split. Still they held, but it it was only a matter of time before the whole roof caved in.

Mace dashed outside. His brother delayed a few seconds to grab hold of his gunbelt. The instinct of the professional gunfighter was never far away. And just as well.

Rocks were now smashing through the weakened roof of the cabin. Most of them had luckily fallen to one side. The rockfall had been relatively small, but it had achieved its purpose of driving the cabin's inhabitants out into the open.

Three rifle shots rang out from the far side of the clearing in quick succession. The first ripped a chunk of wood from the doorpost. But the second struck home. Mace threw up his arms with a cry and tumbled to the ground. He did not get up.

The other was aimed at Clem, but his innate caution kicked in.

Diving headlong through the door of the cabin, he scrambled behind the well. More bullets pinged and whined off its stone rim. The roar of falling rock had now subsided to a growling crackle of split timbers and shifting rocks grinding against each other. Dust rose in clouds, hazing out the bright sunlight.

Clem glanced across at his brother. There was still no movement. He could only assume that Mace was dead.

The bleak thought passed through his mind that a confession from the mayor was no longer required. All that mattered now was that he and the girl should somehow come out of this mess in one piece. Whoever was out there must have been extremely lucky to come across the hidden canyon, or had they somehow been given inside information. Where had he let slip his destination?

Another bullet clipped the rim of the well. Fragments of stone scored a lump out of his cheek. He brushed away the trickle of blood.

This was no place to figure out the whys and wherefores of his predicament. Some jasper was out there trying to kill him. Mace had gone down. And where was Ellie? Had she survived the wrecking of the cabin? Last he'd seen of her was when she went out back to feed the horses. He peered around, but there was no sign of the girl.

Another bullet clanged against the well bucket ricocheting away like an angry hornet. He peered round the edge to try and place where the bushwhacker was hidden. He couldn't reveal himself for fear of being shot. And neither could the bushwhacker. For the time being it was stalemate. Although, in the current situation, the advantage lay with his antagonist.

Once the rockslide had got going, Clark Jarrett picked his way down to the narrow cutting he had spotted. The climb back down to ground level was easy enough, if a touch unstable. Loose gravel was displaced by his boots. Both hands were needed to maintain his footing. He wasn't concerned about the noise because the avalanche effectively drowned out his ungainly descent.

Once he had reached the bottom, which took no more than ten minutes, the narrow rift bent sharply to the left. It was no more than two feet wide and the stocky trickster was forced to sidle along it. Rounding the acute dogleg he came upon the cowering form of Ellie Spavin.

Jarrett recognized her from the Glad Tidings diner. So what in tarnation was she doing out here? Then he remembered that she had been the only person in town to befriend Mace Gifford. They had clearly got together after the escape with the bogus hangman. And now she must have escaped from the avalanche and was also hoping to escape the attack on the cabin.

Too bad for her. She'd failed.

So intent was Ellie on trying to ascertain what was happening at the front of the cabin that Jarrett's catlike approach to her rear had gone unheard.

Lady Luck had seen fit to favour Ellie with her patronage. As soon the avalanche started, she had been outside the cabin with the horses. That she had been directly beneath the overhanging lip of the cliff had saved her life. The deadly rocks plummeting down from above had left her completely unscathed.

Such unexpected disasters are likely to precipitate panic in ordinary mortals. And Ellie was no exception. She had desperately scuttled away along the foot of the cliff from the scene of devastation. Discovering the narrow split in the solid rock wall, she took cover behind a fall of loose scree near the entrance.

Only then did the girl have time to think about the fate of her associates, especially Mace. His brother had certainly proved that he could take care of himself. But her lover was something of a loose cannon, a hothead with a temper.

The crackle of gunfire meant that the cabin and its occupants were under attack. It also suggested that the avalanche had not been a freak of nature.

Ellie felt frustrated and helpless. Swirling clouds of dust prevented her from seeing anything. She had no way of ascertaining the course of the battle being waged in the canyon. Nor how many assailants were out there.

* * *

Clark Jarrett was likewise undecided.

The continuous flurry of gunfire indicated that things were not all going the way that El Camaleon had predicted. The devious mayor of Alamagordo was no hard-boiled gunslick. And he didn't trust the Mexican bandit anyway. He quickly turned over the options in his mind.

He could just slip away before the dust settled. The only thing that stayed his hand was the knowledge that his ill-gotten gains were in that cabin. And Ellie Spavin was the key to retrieving that sack of dough. She was certain to know where it was hidden.

The rear of the cabin had survived the pounding. Viewed from his vantage point to the side, it appeared that the roof and front section had been destroyed. Gingerly, Jarrett drew his pistol and advanced on the unsuspecting girl. The first Ellie knew of the guy's presence was a thick arm encircling her slender neck. A sweaty hand was clamped across her mouth, preventing her crying out for help. A gun barrel was then jammed into her cheek.

Ellie's whole body stiffened. The surprise at being caught off guard soon passed. Thrashing about, she tried to escape by digging her teeth into the assailant's fingers. A yelp from Jarrett was followed by a brutal cuff round the ear which stunned her into silence.

Before she could recover her senses, he untied his necker and gagged her. Then he unfastened the belt around her waist and tied her hands behind her back with it.

'Now listen up, girl,' he snapped, tightening his grip. 'One more trick like that and I'll cut off your ears. You understand me?'

The girl's head nodded.

'Good. Now this is what we're gonna do.'

Quickly, he ordered the girl to take him to the money. As they shuffled back along the edge of the cliff face, Jarrett maintained a tight hold of Ellie's long hair. A few tugs on the flowing locks encouraged her to toe the line.

At the back of the cabin he jerked the girl to a halt and gently pushed open the door with his boot. The room was empty. Clearly, the other occupants were being kept busy at the front. El Camaleon was playing his part to perfection. Jarrett chuckled to himself. The greaser was going to get one heck of a shock if he managed to finish them off.

At that moment, the odds had shifted to an even bet.

'Where's the dough hidden?' Jarrett's rancid breath stung her senses. 'And don't try stalling me. Your pretty life is at stake here. I've killed twice already back in Alamagordo. Another ain't gonna make no difference.'

The girl indicated with a nod of her head a cupboard against the wall to their left. Jarrett pushed Ellie hard in the back. She went sprawling on to the bed.

Jarrett moved across and dragged open the cupboard door. The heavy sack fell out. His eyes blazed with greed as he snatched it up. Ellie tried to make a dash for the open door. But the bonds hampered her. Uttering a feral growl, Jarrett brought the gun barrel down on her head. Blood oozed from a cut on her temple as she fell to the floor.

Outside, the sound of gunfire had faded to an occasional shot.

Jarrett's twisted face broke into a lurid grin of triumph. This was working out better than he could have expected. The greaser's plan had come unstuck. But this was no time for premature self-congratulation. He needed to get away unseen.

He sneaked back out through the rear of the cabin and quickly saddled one of the horses. The pall of ochre dust was beginning to settle. After hooking the sack over the pommel the varmint mounted up. Unused to this strange rider, the horse whinnied and stamped its hoofs. Eventually Jarrett calmed it down but not before the commotion had been overheard by Clem hiding behind the well.

He turned round to see the bulky figure of Clark Jarrett riding away. And the crooked mayor had retrieved the money sack! There was no chance of a pistol shot doing any damage at that distance. Of Ellie there was no sign. Had she also been killed?

Incapable of doing anything trapped in his present situation, Clem could only seethe with indignation as the trickster disappeared into the dusty gloom.

Having reached the tree cover at the far side of the narrow ravine, Jarrett paused for a quick check to see that his duplicity had not been spotted. Satisfied, he gently pressed the horse into motion.

Skirting the edge of the amphitheatre, he soon reached the narrow cleft that gave access to the hidden canyon.

Once out in the open at the far side, a huge sigh of relief hissed from between Jarrett's clenched teeth. His tensed-up muscles relaxed. He had made it.

16

Settling the Score

Another bullet holed the bucket that stood on the edge of the well. Now there were three spouts of water gushing forth. Clem knew that he was in a fix. His mouth was dry from all the dust. Concealed behind a well, he had no chance of escape or getting at the precious fluid without being gunned down.

It was a stand-off. And it was fast becoming clear that the odds were in favour of El Camaleon.

A lilting cadence floated across no man's land.

'Hey Montero, you still there?'

'I'm here and I ain't going nowhere,' was the blunt reply although the assertive tone belied a less than confident speaker. 'And neither are you.'

Another bullet was the Mexican's irritated reaction. Clem laughed out loud. 'Missed again!'

'You cannot escape, bounty man. We have you pinned down. It is only a matter of time before you are dead meat, just like your friend,' called the outlaw, trying to remain unmoved by the verbal exchange. Another couple of rounds whizzed over Clem's head.

'That's my brother you've gunned down,' snarled Clem. 'And for that I aim to see you hang.'

'Ah! Now it becomes clear why you assumed the guise of the hangman.' Esteban's reaction was a hearty guffaw. He found the subterfuge extremely amusing. 'You are another Camaleon, *señor*. I salute you. We are two of a kind, you and I.'

Both adversaries knew that this situation could not go on indefinitely. And the Mexican's newfound respect had given Clem an idea.

'There's something you don't know, *hombre*,' he shouted.

'And what is that?' replied the outlaw.

'That partner of your'n has scarpered and taken the bag of dough with him.'

'You lie, *señor*. It was he started the avalanche.'

'So why has he not made his presence felt?'

There was no answer to that and the Mexican knew it. He had been asking himself the same question. Clem allowed the unwelcome truth to take a firm hold of his opponent's brain before adding, 'I saw him leave with my own eyes.'

'What now then, Montero?' The question was muted, lacking any aggression. The failure of his scheme had knocked the stuffing out of the bandit.

Clem was now ready to make his play. 'We could sit this out and wait for one of us to fall asleep. But that is not the way of *hombres* like us who live by the gun.'

'Have you another suggestion?'

'I say that we settle this man to man,

out in the open.' Clem let the proposition simmer, then he gritted out, 'You ain't scared are you, Camaleon?'

The reaction was just what he had expected.

'Let nobody say that Manuel Esteban of Chihuahua is frightened of anything. Such a slur cannot pass unchallenged. I accept your proposal. Count to three, then we both come out together and walk to the middle of the clearing. No shooting until the chimes on my pocket watch stop. Agreed?'

'Agreed,' Clem called back. He reloaded the Peacemaker.

'*Uno . . . dos . . . tres . . .* '

Both men emerged from hiding. Slowly they stepped out into the open, hands hovering above their holstered six-guns. Each man fastened on to his opponent's every movement, trying to determine the other's gunfighting competence. The distance between them narrowed.

At ten paces the Mexican stopped.

'I see you are wearing the gun you stole from me,' he said. 'It will be my pleasure to take it back when I have killed you.'

'You can try,' sneered Clem.

The Mexican responded to the retort with a mocking smile. Then he extracted the gold watch and laid it down on the ground, all the while keeping a watchful eye on his opponent.

A single click and the tinkling melody was set in motion. Jingling and trilling, the plaintive tune filled the clearing with its lilting rhythm. All other sounds were shut out as the two men concentrated on that one cycle. A minute passed before the chime began to slow down.

Fingers flexed, muscles tensed as both men hunched over, their shoulders lifting slightly. Time stood still in Tomahawk Canyon.

Then, silence.

The Mexican was the first to move. He slapped leather. The gun was halfway out of its holster when he was punched back. A look of total surprise registered on his florid visage. He tottered trying to bring his gun to bear. But all his strength was quickly ebbing away as his life blood poured from the gaping wound in his chest. He sank to his knees, then keeled over on to his back.

Clem walked across and stood over the dying man. Smoke dribbled from the barrel of the gun held at his side.

The Mexican coughed. Blood from a fatally damaged heart pumped out of his mouth. He didn't have much time left.

'I never thought . . . there could be . . . a faster draw than mine . . . gringo,' he gasped. The harsh rasp stuck in his throat.

'My lucky day, greaser,' said Clem.

The dying man laughed at the tit-for-tat insults.

'You catch up with that *traidor*.' The Mexican wearily jabbed a finger at him, 'and give him a bullet from El Camaleon.'

Clem nodded. But there was still something he needed to know before the gunman cashed in his chips.

'Where is he heading?'

Esteban's thick lips flapped open like a landed trout, but nothing emerged. Watery eyes rolled up. He was close to the end. Clem bent down and shook him. It seemed to have the desired effect.

For a brief second the dying bandit rallied, struggling to raise himself on to one elbow. The words hissed out. Slow, measured and barely audible.

'He said . . . something about a fresh start . . . in . . . Tex . . . ' He gave a final sigh, then fell back. Bloodshot eyes glassed over as Manuel Esteban, known as the infamous outlaw El Camaleon, stared sightlessly into the dark portals of eternity.

Clem got back to his feet.

Then suddenly another sound impinged itself on to his consciousness.

It was a groan, coming from behind and to his right, where Mace had fallen.

Euphoria flooded through his aching limbs. His brother was still alive. He hurried across. Carefully lifting the boy into his arms, carried him round to the back of the cabin. The bedroom was still relatively intact, apart from a thick coating of dust.

And there another shock awaited him.

Ellie lay on the bed, her head caked in dried blood. She was struggling to rise, hampered by her bonds. Clem quickly freed her. When she saw whom he was carrying she quickly shook off the numbing effects of her recent assault.

'Is he . . . ?' The words trailed off, fear of the answer bringing a lump to her throat.

'No, he's still breathing,' said Clem, laying the boy down, 'but he's bleeding bad. How are you?'

Gingerly she fingered the gash on her temple, wincing at the touch. 'It's only a cut. I'll live,' she said, noticing Clem's anxious regard for her appearance. 'It probably looks a lot worse that it is.'

Clem gratefully accepted the girl's assurance. 'Can you see to him? I have some unfinished business with a certain town mayor that can't wait.'

The girl waved him away as she hurried across to the badly injured kid.

'You do what has to be done,' she urged him. 'Mace will still need that signed confession after he pulls through.'

Clem hated to leave with his brother in such a dire situation, hovering on the brink. But Ellie seemed confident that she could manage.

* * *

An hour after Clark Jarrett had left Tomahawk Canyon, Clem was hot on his tail. Now that he knew the jasper was heading east for the Texas border it was just a question of urging the paint to a steady gallop.

The trail through Artesia and Hobbs was the most obvious route to take. Clem could only trust that Jarrett would opt for distance from the scene of his skulduggery. Branching off on to some obscure trail would be safer but would likely slow him down. The pursuer was counting on the skunk's expectation that the stand-off in the canyon would continue indefinitely until one or both of the combatants was dead. Preferably both.

What had actually occurred would not have crossed his devious mind in a thousand years.

Clem had just traversed a broad arroyo known as the Penasco Sink when he caught sight of a rising plume of dust some two miles ahead. It appeared to be made by a single rider. Could this be his quarry?

Squeezing more speed out of the paint, he narrowed the distance. Swerving and dodging round clumps of mesquite and organ pipe cacti, the horse flattened its ears as they ploughed onwards.

The level nature of the terrain prevented a furtive approach. And it soon became apparent that the rider had spotted his pursuer. Puffs of white smoke sprang from a pistol as the guy attempted to deter the hunter. The shots went well wide of the intended target. The attempt to stop him reassured Clem that the fugitive must be Clark Jarrett.

He dispatched a couple of shots of his own, just to let the critter know the writing was on the wall.

Round the next hill, Jarrett abandoned his horse and took to the rocks. He settled down to wait for the hunter to appear in his gun sight.

But Clem had read the guy's shifty mind. Leaving the paint ground-hitched on the far side of the craggy outcrop, he grabbed his rifle and shimmied round the back. A jackrabbit scooted out of his way. Two jays perched on a dead tree-branch eyed this strange intruder.

He climbed quickly up a narrow defile and emerged to one side of the waiting bushwhacker on a slab of rock about the size of a small room. It was narrow and slanted down to a four-foot-wide ravine at the back.

Jarrett was leaning out at the front, trying to see what was keeping his intended victim. A frown creased his haggard features. The jasper ought to have appeared by now.

'You looking for me, mister?'

The mayor was lying prone on his stomach on the edge of the low shelf. His body tensed.

'Don't try anything stupid,' Clem rapped, jacking a round up the spout of his rifle to show he meant business. 'You and me have some unfinished business that needs sorting. Now ditch that rifle, then turn around slow and easy like.'

Jarrett swore. He had figured to have got away from Tomahawk Canyon unseen and was idly contemplating how to invest the ten grand once he reached Texas when he caught sight of the pursuer. Now the bastard had got the drop on him.

There was no way that Clark Jarrett intended being dragged back to face a hangman's rope in Alamagordo. His hand tightened on the rifle as he prepared to make his move.

Clem read the cornered varmint's thoughts. The blanching of knuckles tightly clutching the long gun, the surreptitious glance behind, muscles girding up ready for the final count-down. All giveaways that Jarrett was not for surrendering without a fight. But killing the guy was not part of the Clem's plan, at least not until he had signed the confession.

'You don't stand a chance,' he urged the prone figure who was slowly turning to face his captor. 'Give up now and I'll see you get a fair trial.'

Jarrett spat out a harsh laugh.

'Fair trial?' he scoffed. 'Ain't no such thing in Alamagordo. My fate was sealed when I shot that interfering swamper and stole the saloon takings.' He didn't bother to elucidate the details of his most recent iniquity. 'It'll be ignominy and disgrace followed by the hangman's rope if'n I go back there.'

He swung to face his adversary.

'I'm willing to take my chance here.'

Without any further discourse, he raised the rifle and pulled the trigger. But Clem was ready. He threw himself to one side as the bullet from Jarrett's rifle drilled slivers of rock from the boulder to his right. His own gun roared at the same time.

Jarrett was hit in the side. He cried out and dropped the rifle. It was not a killing shot, but packed sufficent power to dislodge the guy from his position, sending him rolling down the slope towards the ravine.

Unable to save himself, Jarrett tumbled over the edge. Luckily he was able to grab hold of a protruding rock.

Clem hurried across and stood over the trembling figure. A sinister smile creased his handsome visage. A raised boot hovered over the mayor's clutching fingers.

'You ready to sign that confession

now?' asked Clem.

A shake of the head from Jarrett. 'Never!'

'Then look down there and see what fate awaits a scumbag like you.'

The wounded man twisted his head; a confused look clouded his blotched face. What he perceived sent a violent shudder through his bulky torso. A whole nest of rattlesnakes were writhing and hissing immediately below his dangling body, attempting to strike at the unwanted interloper.

Jarrett's back arched with terror. Sweat bubbled on his brow.

'No, no!' he exclaimed. Sheer panic gave him the strength to scramble back over the rim of the deadly ravine. But Clem had placed his boot on the guy's head.

'Sign now or join your buddies!' he growled, exerting pressure with his foot. The paper together with a pencil were placed beside the terrified man's clawing hands. 'Sign it!' More pressure forced the victim back over the edge.

His hands began to slip.

'OK, OK, I'll do it. Just keep them ugly critters away,' gasped Jarrett, scrawling his name across the all-important document. Clem smiled and put the paper back into his pocket.

For a brief second he was tempted to push the skunk over the edge anyway. But that was not his way. He had always kept his word in the past. Change now and he would be no better than this piece of dung. Keeping a close watch on the guy, he hauled him up to safety.

Jarrett lay there, panting and shaking, glad to be back on solid ground if only to be put on trial for a double murder. Anything was better than ending his days in that ravine.

Ten minutes later, Clark Jarrett, disgraced mayor of Alamagordo, was tethered and his wound temporarily bandaged up. The two riders headed back for Tomahawk Canyon at a more sedate pace.

There were still questions to be

answered regarding Clem's impersonation of a state hangman, freeing a prisoner due for execution, and assaulting a doctor.

But the bounty hunter known as Montero was confident that bringing in the real culprit would sway any jury in his favour.

More important, there was a certain lady at the Glad Tidings diner with whom he wanted to become far better acquainted in the not too distant future. His brother wasn't the only one who had romance in mind.

THE END

We do hope that you have enjoyed reading this large print book.

Did you know that all of our titles are available for purchase?

We publish a wide range of high quality large print books including:
Romances, Mysteries, Classics
General Fiction
Non Fiction and Westerns

Special interest titles available in large print are:
The Little Oxford Dictionary
Music Book, Song Book
Hymn Book, Service Book

Also available from us courtesy of Oxford University Press:
Young Readers' Dictionary
(large print edition)
Young Readers' Thesaurus
(large print edition)

For further information or a free brochure, please contact us at:
Ulverscroft Large Print Books Ltd.,
The Green, Bradgate Road, Anstey,
Leicester, LE7 7FU, England.
Tel: (00 44) **0116 236 4325**
Fax: (00 44) **0116 234 0205**

Other titles in the
Linford Western Library:

SHADOW OF GUILT

Mark Bannerman

It starts out as a simple mission to trace his kid brother, but Brad Caulderfield rides into trouble when he kills the brother of Marshal Seth Blevins. Charged with murder and pursued by the lawman, Brad has to run for his life. He faces further complications from Stella Goodnight, who is out for his blood when he fails to return her affections. And when his brother reappears, bearing bitter resentments, he is looking headlong into the face of his nemesis . . .